Slater Mountain

The Journey

by Judy Ricketts-White

Mecate Press

an imprint of Ricketts-White Design

Waterford

For Carol Ross – an amazing horseperson, teacher, mentor and friend, who has taught me and the horse study group everything about horses

Slater Mountain Series created by Mecate Press, an imprint of Ricketts-White Design, U.S.A. www.rickettswhitedesign.com

Mecate
Press

ISBN 978-0-9970342-0-2

Library of Congress Control Number: 2015918762

Photo credit for horse on cover: Cowboyway/Dreamstime
Photo credit for girl on cover: Anna Yakimova/Dreamstime
Cover and book design: Judy Ricketts-White

Chapter One

Nugget stood motionless in the pasture, with his ears pricked up, staring beyond the rocks. His eyes were wide as he waited, listening closely. The birds chirped, the breeze blew gently, then he lowered his head and went back to eating grass. He was a large pony, smart and stout in both stature and heart. About then, Bailey Mathews walked into the pasture. Nugget picked up his head again and whinnied. He had been a wild pony when Bailey found him. Living up here in the mountains, she didn't have many friends nearby. She always kept her eyes open for the herd of wild horses that roamed in the area. She and Nugget became friends right away! There was something that just drew them together. They trusted each other.

That was over three years ago, Nugget had been a little more than a yearling then, and traveled with a bachelor band of young stallions. When they met, Bailey was sitting in a meadow working on an agriculture project.

She followed a homeschool program. Living up in the mountains, it was difficult to get to school in town, especially in the wintertime. She lived with her mom and dad, Annie and Will Mathews, her grandpa, Ben Slater and her older brother Ross. Her dad, was away a lot because he worked on the oil rigs in the Gulf of Mexico.

"Hey there boy," Bailey had said at that very first meeting.

Now as Bailey approached him, she said, "Hey there boy, how are you doing?" He nuzzled her arm, and she motioned for him to follow her. "What do you want to do today?" she said, sweeping her light brown hair back into a ponytail. "Mom said I can ride as long as I get my chores and school work done. I finished my school work. After I finish my chores, we can go to the brook and fish for trout. How does that sound?"

By now they had reached the barn. Bailey put Nugget in one of the paddocks. Her mom had three horses at their farm that had been brought there for training. Raina and Chance, both three year-old quarter horses, were there to be started under saddle. Raina was a palomino mare and Chance was a dark bay gelding. Belle was a beautiful bay hunter/jumper who was terribly head shy. The owner had worked with her, but the head shyness was getting worse, not better. Now the owner couldn't even get a bridle on her.

This morning, Bailey had put them out in their paddocks and fed them. Now it was time to feed them again and clean their stalls. She tossed them all some hay, then started on the stalls.

Bailey had figured out that cleaning stalls was a job she didn't have to think about. She liked to put her mind on automatic pilot and use the time to plan a project, think about her afternoon ride, or anything she wanted.

As Bailey cleaned the stalls, she thought about how amazing horses are. "Horses don't really have a spoken language, they only make a few sounds. A whinny tells others, 'I'm here,' a nicker says, 'come to me,' a snort announces danger, and a squeal is sounded usually right before a strike. They say almost everything else with their body language," Bailey thought. "I'm so lucky that Mom and Grandpa are teaching me to understand the way horses communicate. Learning to 'speak' horse is way more fun than learning French or Spanish."

When she was finished with the stalls, Bailey brought Nugget in from the paddock. Bailey picked up a brush and gave him a good grooming. He had been rolling and had some stick-tights in his mane.

She hoisted the saddle pad onto his back and then the saddle and gently cinched it up. Bailey always made sure that Nugget was okay with every step of the tacking-up process before she continued. If he gave her any hint (with his body language), that he was not happy with whatever was happening, she would wait or work with him to make sure that he was relaxed.

Her mom and grandpa had shown her how to work around horses. She had learned to ride on her pony Lucy, then on an older bombproof horse Moses. Moses *really* was bombproof. He would do anything asked of him and literally didn't care. Annie Mathews had started Nugget under saddle last year. As Annie worked with Nugget and he became more dependable, Bailey rode him more and more. Bailey cleaned out Nugget's hooves and checked him over carefully. She moved Nugget around on the ground for a bit to make sure he was listening to her. As she fastened the fishing gear to the saddle, her mom walked by leading Raina toward the round pen.

"Where are you heading?" Annie asked.

"To the brook to go fishing," grinned Bailey.

"Yum, trout for dinner," quipped Annie. I'm going to work Raina and Chance, want to watch? You can go fishing in a little while."

"Sure," replied Bailey. She hardly ever missed an

opportunity to watch her mom work a horse.

"You can soft tie Nugget to the outside of the round pen." her mom suggested.

"Okay." Bailey said as she removed Nugget's bridle and put on his halter and lead rope. Then she wrapped the lead rope three times around one of the horizontal bars of the pen. She didn't tie the rope, just let the end hang down.

Annie reminded her, "that way the rope has some drag, but slips. If the horse pulls back, he won't panic, because the rope will slide. If the horse is hard tied and pulls back, he could panic, break the halter, or flip over and hurt himself. Soft tying actually helps the horse teach himself to give to pressure by coming forward."

Annie led Raina into the round pen, and removed her halter and lead rope. "I'm going to establish forward motion first," she said, as she sent the horse out circling to the left. "I don't care whether Raina walks, trots or lopes, only that she moves forward and keeps moving to the left."

Bailey loved how her mom always described what she was doing as she did it. Annie also pointed out what the horse was doing in her body language and even sometimes what she thought the horse was thinking.

Raina started trotting, went into a lope, then came back to a trot. Annie explained, "I'm not asking for a faster gait. I'm only directing my energy behind her driveline, in back of her front leg and asking for forward. Since Raina slowed her gait, I'm lowering my energy, so eventually my energy will mean something to her. Now I will ask her to change her direction by turning toward me. I'll use my body language by backing up to release pressure and draw her toward me. If she doesn't come toward me, I can use pressure on her hind end. Her head is starting to lower a bit, this is a sign of relaxation. See how she's starting to pay more attention to me. Her inside ear is turned toward me almost all the time now. I back, she slows and stops, and then slightly turns toward me, I back a little more to draw her. I don't want her turning away from me, as that would encourage her to leave me and I don't ever want my horse to leave me."

Even though Raina was an emotional horse, the session went smoothly. Annie's clear and consistent method of communication while moving the horse's feet provided leadership and calmed the horse.

"Great session, Mom," Bailey said. "Toward the end, Raina was using the thinking side of her brain more than the reactive side."

"Good observation," Annie remarked, while letting Raina rest, standing quietly. "Yes, she's progressing nicely. See how much having Nugget soft tied to the round pen helped her?" Annie said, as she brought Raina out of the pen. "It also teaches Nugget patience."

"He looks pretty patient to me!" laughed Bailey, as she scratched behind Nugget's ear while he was dozing in the sun.

"Nugget truly is turning out to be a great horse, he's getting more broke every day! Would you take Raina to her paddock and bring Chance to me? I'll keep an eye on Nugget," Annie said, then she took a big drink of water.

"I gave Raina some hay," Bailey said a few minutes later, handing Chance's lead to Annie.

"This fella seems to be more confident than Raina. He's definitely a thinker," Annie said, while repeating the same process with Chance. "See how he's expressing a little attitude when I ask him to move? I still have to start soft, he's just as sensitive as Raina, but I have to be ready to back it up with stronger pressure and more energy if needed. I'm walking a smaller circle than Chance is, keeping my energy focused behind his driveline. It's almost like there's an invisible rope attached from me to him. If his front end starts to come in and I don't want it to, I turn my energy and focus on his shoulder and front end till it moves away. I put my focus and energy on whatever part of the horse I want to move."

"Wow, Mom, it's a lot to take in," Bailey sighed.

"You almost do this naturally, you're so sensitive

and intuitive. I'm putting it into words to help you understand." Annie explained. "I always want to be having a conversation with my horse. I have to be the same way with my horse all the time, whether I'm leading, working in the round pen or riding."

"I guess I'm not that way all the time with my horse," Bailey admitted .

"You're doing great, honey," Annie reassured her. "You're so far ahead of where I was at your age. You only just turned fifteen, be aware, be patient and keep working at it."

"Thanks, Mom, I love you," beamed Bailey.

"Please take Chance and bring out Belle. I need to check out all the basics with her before I start working on her head shy issue."

"Here she is, Mom. What a pretty girl," Bailey said a few minutes later, as she brought Belle out and handed the lead rope to Annie.

"Yes, she is pretty," Annie replied. "Let's see how she does."

Annie asked Belle to move off to the right. Belle immediately spun and kicked out as she moved out.

"Woo," said Annie. "She's definitely got some energy. We'll watch her. See how she's looking outside the round pen? She has absolutely no interest in me. I'm not asking her to canter, that's her choice. I'm going to match her energy and keep her cantering, because then I'm controlling her feet. I will do this until she shows some sign of being interested in me. There's no way I could work on her head issues without having her attention and establishing a means of communicating with her. Right now, she might try to slow down, bring her head from looking outside to straight or inside, put an ear on me or lower her head a bit. Any of these things are a sign that she might be ready to communicate."

"Is there any way to make this happen faster? Bailey asked.

"Sometimes," Annie replied, "but I've learned that usually the best way is to set it up for the horse and let her find the answer. It may not be the fastest way, but the horse chooses the answer, so they learn, and won't forget. This way helps the horse learn how to learn, and to search for the answer. See there, she just put an ear on me. I think she wants to slow down, so I'm lowering my energy and allowing her to slow to a trot as a reward for paying attention to me. She slowed, she's looking at me, so I'm backing slightly to allow her to stop. She's stopped and is still looking at me, so I back just a little more and she turns and takes one step toward me, perfect."

"Belle's responses really looked nice, Mom," said Bailey.

"Now I'm going to repeat this going to the left," Annie said. "Then we'll be done for the day."

It took slightly less time for Belle as Annie repeated the process on the left side.

"I'm going to head for the brook," Bailey said as she switched out Nugget's halter for the bridle. "Mom, can I get my own phone?" she asked. "It would make it so much easier to keep in touch with you, especially when I'm riding...and of course with my friends too."

"Your dad and I will have to talk about it when he gets home," Annie replied. "Don't be too long, I'm getting hungry already."

"I'll be back in a little while," Bailey called out, as she checked Nugget's cinch and made sure the fishing gear was secure. Bailey hopped into the saddle. She waited for a few minutes rubbing Nugget's neck and withers, then she asked him to walk by raising her body energy. He quietly walked off as she squeezed gently with both calves. "Good boy," Bailey said in a soft voice.

The ride to the brook was a couple miles. There was a stream closer to the house, but Carson Brook was bigger, and was great for catching trout.

When they arrived at the water's edge, Bailey swung her leg down from the saddle. It was so beautiful there. The sounds gurgled downstream as the water danced happily over the rocks. The sunlight filtered through the trees as Bailey dug some worms from the muddy area between the glade and the brook. Bailey baited the hook and cast into the middle, where the water was calm. While she waited for a nibble, Nugget grazed contentedly on grass in the nearby glade.

Even though Bailey loved being with people, she also enjoyed time by herself. Some of her best experiences happened when she was on her own.

"Aha," she chirped, as she felt a nibble and set the hook. Slowly she reeled in the trout, as she said, "Grandpa will love cooking you up for dinner tonight!" After she had caught a few more fish, she and Nugget drank some fresh, cold water from the brook. Then they headed home.

"We haven't had trout to eat in quite a while," Grandpa said. They all enjoyed the tasty grilled fish with a fresh salad made from their garden.

During dinner, Bailey asked her mom, "Why do you think Nugget chose to approach us in the field that day two years ago?"

"From what you described to me, it sounds like the herd was constantly rejecting him," Annie explained. "That made him low man in the pecking order. The lead stallion pushed him to the outside edge of the herd, which is the most dangerous place to be if predators attack. When he saw you and Moses in the field, he might have sensed a welcoming feeling. Maybe he just felt the lack of negative energy that he had been constantly feeling in his herd, we'll never know for sure. Whatever the reason was, he became curious enough to investigate "this other herd," you and Moses. Somehow, Nugget felt safer with you two than with the bachelor band."

"I'm so happy Nugget came to us. I can't imagine him not being here," Bailey sighed, smiling and close to tears, all at the same time.

"Well, honey, you and Moses have a great bond and Nugget wanted to be part of that feeling," Annie commented.

"Do you think this has happened before with wild horses?" asked Bailey.

"Many years ago," Ben began, "I heard about a rancher, not far from here, that found a wild stallion with his leg caught in barbed wire. The horse was hurt pretty bad. He managed to free the horse. The horse couldn't really run. The man healed up the horse's leg and they made a connection. Even after the horse was healed, he never ran away. The horse stayed with old Mike the rest of his life."

"Most of the time, wild horses were either roped or herded into pens," Ben continued. I've never heard of anything like what happened with you, Moses and Nugget. A wild horse willingly joining a human and a broke horse—the way I see it, that's something pretty special."

Bailey jumped out of bed the next morning eager to start the day. Her best friend Charlie Anderson was coming over. Bailey wanted to get her school work and chores done early so they could watch her mom work horses. Afterward, Annie was giving the two girls a riding lesson together.

"You're up early," Annie smiled.

"Charlie's coming today so we can watch you work the horses and then we're having our lesson!" Bailey bubbled with anticipation.

"It's going to be a fun day," Annie grinned. What do you want to eat?"

"I'll have fruit and yogurt, please," answered Bailey.

"Toast too?" Annie queried.

"Yes, thanks," said Bailey, gobbling down the yogurt, grabbing a banana and the toast, and flying out the door.

"Don't forget your school work!" hollered Annie.

Bailey sat on a hay bale and finished her breakfast, while she planned her attack on the chores. She put the horses there for training out first, did the feeding, then decided to clean stalls. Once finished, she tacked up Nugget and rode to the meadow to work on her school project.

Bailey sat in the meadow waiting for the wild

horses to come through. Nugget munched on grass close by. She was working on her notes documenting her observations of the wild horses, and started thinking about when she met Nugget.

That day, she was sitting in this same field working on her school project comparing different types of pasture grasses, when she saw the herd moving on the edge of the meadow. She started noticing the colors and sizes of the horses and watched how they interacted with each other. The idea came to Bailey to do a school project documenting these horses. Bailey tried not to seem interested in them, she didn't look directly at them. She started going to the field every day. She sat and worked on the pasture grasses project and made notes about the horses, and waited. She brought her camera and notebook, and waited. Somedays she would see them, other days she wouldn't. Then the horses started coming almost every day.

This most northern pasture was actually two pastures. It was divided by an area of trees just about in the center, growing into the field on both sides forming a natural border between the two fields. The trees didn't connect completely, creating almost a gate-like gap to move from one field to the other.

Back then, Bailey always rode Moses and he would contentedly much on grass while she would sit and work on her wild horse herd project. She and

Moses stayed in the southern-most field (of the two fields) and when the wild horses came through, the horses would be in the northern field.

The main herd of mares, foals and one stallion traveled through first and a bachelor band would come in a little while after the main herd had moved out of the area.

Bailey gave each horse a name, mostly based on color or markings, such as Blaze for the sorrel lead mare with a white blaze, and Roanie for the main herd stallion who was a red roan. The main heard always kept a good distance away from Bailey and Moses. Bailey figured they were protecting the foals. The bachelor band, however, was more curious. They approached the opening between the two fields and started hanging around barely on the inside of the field where Bailey and Moses were pretending to ignore them. The young stallions seemed at ease munching the grass. The leader, a big bay stallion, kept pushing Nugget to the outside of the group. Eventually, he just stayed on the edge of the bachelor band. Nugget mostly trailed behind, the most dangerous place to be for a member of a wild herd. This is the place predators can easily pick off stragglers.

This continued for weeks until finally one day, Nugget started moving closer to Bailey and Moses. The other wild horses stayed closer to the opening, but Nugget slowly approached moving back and forth in a zigzag pattern, stopping to graze but keeping an eye on them and staying alert. Bailey kept her gaze and body slightly turned away from Nugget. She watched Moses who was relaxed and grazed contently. Moses picked his head up and softly looked at Nugget, then casually went back to munching grass. Moses must have already known that Nugget was not a threat and had actually welcomed him.

Bailey kept thinking thoughts of love, breathing slowly and calmly. She kept looking at Moses who acted like nothing unusual was happening. It seemed like that moment stretched out forever, time seemed almost suspended. The sun beat down on them. The warm breeze blew gently making the grasses flow in fluid wave patterns back and forth across and the entire length of the field. Bailey felt beads of sweat on her upper lip. A butterfly landed on the head of a stalk of grass in front of her. Bailey felt almost afraid to breathe, but kept breathing slowly and calmly. Then as if he had always been there, Nugget was there grazing along side them, right with them.

In the days that followed, Bailey took a halter, lead rope and brush to the field. When the wild horses would come through, she would always wait for Nugget to approach her. She didn't approach him. She gently brushed him and rubbed the rope all over him until she could put the halter and lead rope on him. She led him around the field and then ponied him while riding Moses. Bailey named him Nugget because he was a buckskin, golden in color, with a thick dark mane and tail. Mining had been done in the mountains many years ago, and now all the mines were abandoned. She felt that he was the nugget of gold that she found on the mountain.

The three of them had become good friends and one day she just ponied Nugget home. Bailey couldn't believe that happened two years ago, it seemed like yesterday.

Bailey was roused from her daydream by the sounds of the wild horses. She was always in awe at the sight of them, the way they moved, almost as if they were one being, without any outward signs of communicating with each other. It seemed like they used mental telepathy, but Bailey's mom had taught her that they read each other's energy and body language.

Bailey observed them and made notes in her notebook. Blaze was leading, then two other mares, Midnight and Star, followed up by two colts, Four Sox and Snip and a small filly, Little Star. Bailey noticed that two other mares, Brownie and Dawn had bite marks on their rumps and backs. They were followed by two other fillies, Mocha and Graycie.

Bailey laughed to herself as Four Sox and Snip

chased each other around and around. They kicked up their heels, pinned their ears and snaked their heads at each other and then dove down to the ground and rolled. Finally they settled down and started to eat grass with the rest of the herd.

Bailey took some photos and made more notes. Five foals had been born and survived that she had seen in the last two years. Three last year and two this year. Last year's foals were just about full grown, two colts and a filly. Bailey made sure that she got some photos of the bite marks on Brownie and Dawn and of Four Sox and Snip playing.

Bailey rode Nugget, and ponied Moses to the field today. For about the first year after her mom started Nugget under saddle, she had ridden Moses and ponied Nugget. Moses had a calming effect on any situation, and helped keep Nugget anchored to their herd of three. Her mom insisted that she bring Moses. Moses obviously played a huge part in why Nugget decided to join them two years ago. Moses was a very unique horse. He was a leader that didn't seem at all like most horse leaders. Moses was like a wise sage, a quiet pond, soothing and refreshing. He didn't obviously try to boss other horses around, yet they all wanted to be with him. If there was a disagreement about to boil over between two horses, all Moses had to do was quietly walk near them and they immediately stopped and dispersed. Any horse being chased by another would often run to where Moses was, knowing the second horse would stop when they got close.

Moses was a safe refuge in the herd at the farm, just as he had become a safe refuge for Nugget even in the wild. Bailey liked to think that she too had become part of that safe herd for Nugget.

Bailey had an affinity for all animals, but she had a special connection with horses. Horses played a part in Bailey's life every single day, and that was exactly how she wanted her life to be.

Chapter Two

When Bailey, Moses and Nugget arrived back at the barn, her brother Ross and Grandpa had just gotten back from the west pasture.

"Did you find all the missing sheep?" Bailey asked.

"Yes, we managed to get every last one of them in and fixed the fence too," Grandpa hollered out, as he dismounted and gave his horse Rusty a rub. "Good boy, Rusty, you did a good day's work today."

"Why those sheep wanted to be in the brambles is a mystery to me," Ross grimaced as he dismounted. "I cut myself good in those brambles and ripped a perfectly good pair of jeans. I should wash these cuts and put some antiseptic on them. I better check Hondo's legs for cuts, too."

"Good idea, Ross," Annie said. "We don't need anyone, human or animal getting infections.

"That's for sure," declared Ben.

Bailey put Nugget in a paddock, removed his bridle, loosened his cinch a bit and made sure he had some water.

Charlie rode in on her horse, Scooter, and dismounted. "Hi, Mrs. Mathews," Charlie said. "Want me to go get one of the horses?"

"Sure, Charlie," Annie replied. "Bring Raina out first."

"Okay, I'll fetch her," said Charlie, as she soft tied Scooter to the round pen with her "get down rope."

"I'll get Scooter some water," said Bailey.

"Great, thanks! Watching horses get worked and having a riding lesson all in the same day, I'm loving it!" said Charlie.

Charlie brought Raina out and Annie repeated the same program as the day before.

"Since she's doing so well, I'm going to work a little more on the inside turns," Annie explained as she waited for Raina's ear to be on her. Then Annie backed up and drew Raina to her. When Raina came to her, she put pressure on her front end to turn, then pressure for her to move out in the opposite direction. The inside turn was completed and Raina was moving off again in the opposite direction.

"Yay, Mom," Bailey called out. "That was beautiful! Raina's really getting it."

"I'm going to work Raina a little bit longer, then put her up, because she's making such good progress," Annie decided. "That way she'll have plenty of soak time before the next session." After a few more inside turns, Annie brought Raina in. "That should do it for today," she said rubbing Raina gently on the forehead.

"I'll put Raina in her stall and get Chance," Bailey said, grabbing the lead from Annie.

Annie repeated the same process with Chance. This session went extremely well also.

"Okay girls, put Chance in his stall and mount up for your lesson." Annie said, handing Chance off to Bailey and getting a big drink of water. "Let's move to the arena, both of you will ride together."

"I want you both to warm up a little by walking to the left on the rail, Annie said. "Ride on the buckle or completely loose rein. If your horse comes off the rail simply pick up the outside rein gently and guide him back to the rail. The second he heads for the rail, drop the rein. Good, that looks good. Now as you approach the center of the long side, turn and cut through the center, go to the opposite rail and change directions. Now repeat this moving to the right. Remember to keep your eyes up looking always where you want to go, good. Continue this for another lap around."

"Is this right, Mrs. Mathews?" asked Charlie.

"Yes, perfect," Annie responded.

"When your horse comes off the rail, put your inside leg on, wait for a response then pick up the outside rein and gently guide him back to the rail. The second he moves toward the rail release any leg pressure and drop the rein. That's good."

"Like this?" Bailey asked.

"Yes, that looks great," Annie answered.

"Eventually, your horse will start to move back to the rail when you put your leg on. You're teaching him to respond to your leg before you even use your rein."

"That's so cool, Mom," Bailey said excitedly.

"Okay, now let's ask for a trot and repeat the same exercise. First use only your outside rein to bring him back to the rail. Now put your inside leg on, wait for a response, then pick up the outside rein and bring him gently back to the rail. Good, when you approach the center of the long side, turn and change directions. Now repeat the same exercise moving in the new direction at a trot. You both are doing an excellent job. Circle once more at a trot then come back to a walk and let them totally relax, but keep them on the rail. Good work. We'll try it again next lesson and try it at the lope too."

"Thanks, Mom," Bailey said. "That was a super lesson. Charlie and I are going for a ride. Think I'll ride Moses since I rode Nugget for the lesson."

"Okay, don't be too late. Charlie, do you want to stay for dinner?" Annie asked.

"No thanks, Mrs. Mathews," replied Charlie. "My mom wants me home for dinner."

Bailey and Charlie rode toward Carson brook. It was a beautiful sunny day. They decided to ride in the big open field right before arriving at the brook. The grass was green and gold, and glistened in the sunlight. They rode a little while at a walk, trot and canter. Bailey pulled a length of rope off her saddle.

"Let's use the rope to see if we can stay beside each other," Bailey suggested.

"Sounds like fun!" Charlie smiled.

"Let's start with about four feet of rope between us at a walk," Bailey said, handing Charlie one end of the rope, then moving away a few feet.

As they walked, they talked and laughed. They made turns and changed directions while not allowing the rope to pull out of their hands.

"We're doing pretty good," said Charlie. "Let's try it at a trot."

"Okay, one, two, three, trot," Bailey said, and they

picked up the trot.

"Ooohweee!" squealed Charlie. "This is harder."

"We have to stay synchronized," said Bailey.

"I'm having to rate Scooter," said Charlie. "He has a slightly bigger trot than Moses."

"I'm having to speed Moses up a bit," Bailey said, "trying to keep up to Scooter."

"Let's use our legs to keep them at the right distance apart," Charlie said excitedly.

"Like Mom was teaching us in the lesson," Bailey added.

"Whoops!" Charlie hollered and laughed as the rope slid out of her hand. "Let's try that again!"

"Hey, we're doing really good now," Bailey laughed.

"Yeah, we've got it!" Charlie chuckled.

"Let's go back to the walk and shorten the rope," Bailey suggested.

"This is so much fun!" Charlie grinned.

"We'll see how this goes," Bailey smiled.

"Hey, we're in the zone," Charlie said in a quirky way.

"Okay, let's step it up to a trot," Bailey nodded.

"Hey, that wasn't so great," they both giggled as the rope popped out of Bailey's hand. "Do over, do over," they were both still giggling.

"Let's try it one more time," Charlie said.

"Now we're doing better," Bailey said. Then Moses

stumbled and Bailey had to let go of the rope. "Are you okay boy?"

"Look what time it is," Charlie said, looking at her phone. "We better go. I've got to get home."

"You go ahead," Bailey said. "I'm going to take it slower, Moses seems a bit sore."

Charlie made a beeline back toward Bailey's house and Bailey followed at a slower pace. Bailey saw Ross working and rode up to him.

"Ross, will you check Moses' left front leg?" Bailey asked. "He stumbled when Charlie and I were riding and seems sore."

"Sure, hop off," Ross said. "He's definitely a little swollen in his pastern area, right here. Let's put a cold wrap on him."

"See, he's limping a bit," Bailey said, as they headed for the barn.

"Put the cold wrap on now for 20 minutes, and again for 20 minutes before you go to bed," Ross suggested.

"I will," said Bailey. "Will you check him with me later?"

"I'd be glad to," Ross agreed.

"Ross and I are leaving tomorrow morning for the clinic in Baxter, before you and Bailey get up,"

Annie said to Grandpa at dinner that night. "After dinner, I could use everyone's help to get everything packed in the trailer and ready to leave."

Grandpa nodded, and Ross and Bailey said, "Sure, Mom."

"In the morning all Ross and I will have to do is load Smokey and Hondo and get on the road," Annie added. "We have to get to bed early," Annie said to Ross.

"Bailey you'll be helping Grandpa with all the chores and keeping up with your schoolwork while we're gone," Annie stated.

"Yes, Mom, I can do it," Bailey said.

First thing in the morning, Bailey went to the barn to check Moses' leg. The night before, she and Ross decided to put Moses in a stall to help him rest his leg and keep him from injuring it worse.

"How's that leg feeling today?" Bailey asked softly. It looked a little less swollen to her, as she gently felt down his leg. "Oh, it's looking much better, boy," Bailey said, as she put the cold wrap on him. "Another day or two and you'll be feeling as good as ever." She hugged his neck and gently stroked his forelock. "I'll check on you in a little while," she said, as she gave him his grain and placed his hay in the stall.

The next day and the following day, Bailey filled with work on her school projects, chores and meals with her grandpa. She managed to squeeze in a ride with Charlie in the afternoon.

Later that evening the wind began to blow, it started raining, then rained very hard. During the night Bailey heard the wind howling, storms were pretty tough up on the mountain.

Bailey was jolted awake with a huge *crack, bang*! "What was that?'" she yelled. Now she was wide awake! She jumped out of bed and threw on her clothes. She ran through the house shouting, "Grandpa, Grandpa, where are you?" There was no answer. It was barely getting light now. "Grandpa, Grandpa!" Again, there was no answer.

Now she was outside and ran toward the barn. She could almost see clearly. The big pine tree near the barn was down. It must have been blown over by the fierce winds. "Grandpa, Grandpa," she called again.

"Over here," she heard her grandpa's voice. His voice sounded weak.

She didn't see him. She saw the gigantic roots pulled right out of the ground and the huge trunk. "Grandpa, where are you?"

"Here, Bailey," Ben called.

Finally, she saw him. His head was sticking out from under some of the branches. "Oh, Grandpa, are you okay?" she asked.

"I'm not sure, I'm stuck, and my leg hurts," moaned Ben.

"Can you move?" asked Bailey.

"I can move my arms and one leg, but the other leg is pinned. My head hurts too," replied Ben.

"What should I do?" asked Bailey.

"Tack up Moses and bring him over with a long rope. Maybe together you can pull the branch just enough to get me free," he suggested.

"I'll have to use Nugget, Moses' leg is still swollen. I'll be right back," she answered.

She caught Nugget, tacked him up and found a good strong rope. She backed Nugget up to the tree, looped one end of the rope around the branch that was pinning her grandpa's leg and the other end around the saddle horn. Then she stopped to let the little horse settle. All the while, she had been moving fast because she needed to help her grandpa, but she knew she needed to stay calm and not get Nugget rattled.

"That's good," said Ben. "Now slowly and gently ask him to walk forward just enough to take the slack out of the rope. That's it. Let him feel the weight of the taut rope. Now back him slightly to let the tension off the rope so he knows you will give him a release. That's good. Now slowly walk him forward again a little at a time," he directed her.

"Like this, Grandpa?" she asked.

"Yes, great," he said. "I can feel some pressure coming off my leg. Keep going slowly, almost there. I think I can drag myself clear. I'm free. Now, back him up slowly, just enough to create slack in the rope again." Bailey did exactly what Ben told her to do. Then she removed the rope. "Great work, Bailey!" Ben said, his voice trailing off.

"Are you okay, Grandpa?" Bailey was worried. Her grandpa looked exhausted.

"I think my leg is broken," replied Ben. I can't stand up," he stated.

Bailey was by his side. "You've got a cut and a bump on your head too," she noticed. She went to the house, got scissors, a cold wet cloth, antiseptic and bandages. She washed his head, put on antiseptic and a band-aid. Then she cut his pant leg with the scissors and looked at his leg. His lower leg was very swollen and discolored, but the skin was not broken.

Everyone in Bailey's family had training in basic first aid, but this was beyond what the two of them could handle.

"We need to get help," they both said at the same time.

"Where's your cell phone?" She asked.

"It's not in my pocket," said Ben, feeling his pockets. Then he tried to feel the ground around himself with his hands, but found nothing.

Bailey searched the area where her grandpa had been trapped under the tree. Finally, she saw it and picked it up. "It must have broken when you were thrown to the ground," Bailey said out loud.

"How about using the computer?" Grandpa suggested.

Bailey ran into the house and came running back out a few minutes later. "I can't get online, Grandpa," she sighed. "Did the storm do that too?"

"Look the tree took out the satellite dish too," Ben observed.

"What are we going to do now?" she asked, as they looked at each other. "I can ride Nugget down the mountain road to the Anderson's and get help," Bailey suggested.

"That sounds like the best option," Ben agreed.

She checked Nugget's tack, hopped into the saddle and set off down the mountain road. She had only gone a mile and a half when she saw a rock slide and trees down, completely blocking the pass. "What are we going to do now, Nugget?" she gasped. "There's no way through or around." She turned around and headed home.

"Grandpa, there's a rock slide blocking the pass and there's no way around it," she grimaced, once she reached his side again.

"Take the trail along Wilburn Creek to Mrs. Collins's place. It's a long trail and way off the track, but Sarah will either have a phone or will be able to get you to a phone."

"Grandpa, I'm scared, I've never been that direction in the back country by myself."

"Honey, I need help and it seems the only way," Ben said encouraging her. "You can do it. You're strong, smart and have great horse skills. If you get into trouble, talk to God, he is always there to help you," Ben said reassuring her.

"You always say just what I need to hear," she said hugging him.

"How far is it to the Collins's place?" Bailey asked.

"I think about five or six miles. Stay along the creek for as long as you can, probably about three or four miles, then take the left trail. There will be some other paths, but stay on the main trail until you reach a grove of pine trees, then take the right trail. That should take you all the way to Sarah's house," Ben explained.

Bailey went into the house and came out with two canteens filled with water, a sandwich and a blanket. She put the blanket over her grandpa, gave him one canteen and a kiss. Ben didn't want anything to eat because he thought he might have a concussion. She took the other canteen, the sandwich and readied herself to set out again. "I'll get help to you as soon as I can," she promised.

"Wear your helmet to be safe," Ben hollered.

"Got it," Bailey hollered back, as she ran to get her helmet. She put it on, mounted up again and loped off down the driveway.

Chapter Three

As Bailey headed back down the mountain road, she couldn't help but think about her grandpa. She was worried because he was in pain and he looked so exhausted. She knew how important it was to get him help as soon as she could.

Bailey turned Nugget onto the trail at Wilburn Creek. She knew trotting would be faster, but the trail was so rocky and uneven she didn't want to risk Nugget tripping, falling or getting injured. They walked most of the time. Bailey would give him a little squeeze with her legs to ask him to trot for a bit whenever the trail evened out. At one point, she stopped to let Nugget drink from the creek. She was hungry so she ate her sandwich. When she thought they'd gone a couple miles, she started looking for the left trail turn-off.

Suddenly there was a loud *crack*, followed by a

boom. Nugget jumped sideways and then spread all four feet and stuck low to the ground, like a leopard would land after jumping out of a tree. All this happened in a split second before Bailey could even think about what the noise was. By now, Nugget was standing quiet and relaxed, and turned almost all the way around facing the direction they had come. Bailey turned the rest of the way to see the big tree limb that broke and landed on the ground right behind them. Now the limb was almost in front of them. "Whew, that was close!" she exclaimed, very happy that the limb missed them completely.

"It's a good thing we practiced our one-rein stops, even though you didn't run far and we didn't have to use it," she told Nugget. Bailey had an "Aha moment" realizing there was a reason for all the things her mom and grandpa taught her about horses – "and about life," she spoke the last part out loud and then laughed, because she thought she was thinking to herself. Now she knew all the practice helped Nugget to know he could calm himself quickly without having to run very far when he got scared. The practice also helped her know what to do in case Nugget had bolted down the trail.

Bailey and Nugget continued on. A little further down the trail, three does kicked up and crossed the trail fairly close in front of them. Nugget's head came up quickly and he spooked in place. Bailey heard and saw the deer moving across the trail, but she stayed calm and watched them cross the creek and disappear into the woods. The deer startled Nugget a little, he was alert as he watched them. Luckily being raised in the wild, he was used to seeing deer. When Nugget was relaxed and his head lowered again, Bailey rubbed his neck. "Good boy," she said softly.

As Bailey and Nugget continued walking, the sun sparkled through the leaves. Dragonflies and bugs flitted back and forth across the creek and birds chirped. Bailey listened to the sound of the creek as it skipped, swished and flowed along side them. Even though it was a peaceful ride, the thought never left her mind that she was on an important mission.

After another mile or so, Bailey spotted the left trail turn-off. She and Nugget turned onto the new track heading away from the creek. The trail became flat and even, so she picked Nugget up to a trot. She felt like she was really making progress now. Bailey loved the way Nugget's trot was so balanced and comfortable to ride. They settled into a nice gentle rhythm and she posted to help take any stress off Nugget's back.

Bailey saw a curve up ahead. As they came around the curve she saw a huge tree down blocking the trail. It must have blown down during the storm. On the left side was a rock ledge going almost

straight up that began quite a distance back and continued on. On the right side were brambles and a
dense thicket. Bailey couldn't see any way around the
downed tree, and it was pretty high. Nugget wouldn't
be able to step over it.

Bailey slowly approached the tree trunk and she
and Nugget looked over it. The top of the trunk
came up to his chest. "What do you think, boy? Do
you think we can jump it?" Bailey asked, rubbing his
neck gently. She had never jumped anything this
high before while riding Nugget. "I know, we've gone
over ground poles and low cavaletti jumps, but nothing this big!" Bailey let out a sigh. She sighed again
and said, "It looks like we're going to have to jump it,
boy!"

Bailey walked Nugget up to the tree again, and let
him investigate it. He sniffed it, pawed at the ground
in front of it and looked over it. Nugget's ears were
flicking back and forth. He was looking forward
alert and checking things out, then his ears turned
backward, he was paying attention to Bailey. Bailey
checked out the trail on the other side, it looked
clear.

Nugget's ears turned back on her again, he was
asking Bailey, "What do you want me to do?"

She backed him up, and walked up to the tree
again. This time she urged him even closer so his
chest and legs touched the tree. He tried to put a

hoof up and pawed higher on the trunk. Then Nugget put his head over and looked at the ground on the other side. As they were investigating, Bailey let him know that he was doing exactly what she wanted him to do. "Good boy," she said calmly as she rubbed his neck. She wanted him to know everything about this tree, how tall and wide it was, and that the ground was safe where he would have to take off and land.

This time she backed him up further and trotted to the tree, slowing before arriving at the trunk. She stopped and let him check it out some more. Bailey backed him quite a distance this time and took off at a lope, slowing before they reached the tree. Again, she let Nugget check out the tree.

"Well, I guess this is it, buddy," she sighed and took a deep breath, both scared and excited all at the same time.

Bailey cued Nugget and they took off at a lope. As they approached the tree, she took the jumping position and cued him strongly a couple times. She looked up, over and far beyond the trunk, saying, "Yes, Nugget, we're going over!"

Bailey felt his body spring and rise beneath her. She held the reins loosely and had her hands holding his mane so she wouldn't pull on his mouth. They flew through the air together and landed safely on the far side of the tree. She continued to lope Nugget for a few strides then adjusted her seat to slow him to a trot and then a walk. Bailey softly rubbed his neck. "Good boy, Nugget," she said. "Let's go get help for Grandpa."

Bailey and Nugget continued down the trail. When it was smooth and even, they would trot. When it was rocky and uneven they would walk. Bailey could smell the dampness in the air and earth from last night's storm as they rode. She watched as two squirrels skittered up a tree and jumped branches to the next tree darting and playing as they went. Until now she had been traveling up and down small inclines, but mostly uphill. The sun was much higher now in the sky and was barely visible peeking through some left-over clouds. They stopped at a small creek for a quick drink, then continued on.

"How you doing, boy?" Bailey asked Nugget while gently rubbing his neck. Nugget's ear flicked front to back and front to back again, as he paid attention to the trail ahead and listened to Bailey. "I think we're making good time. Hope we get to the pine grove soon," she said adjusting her helmet and shifting her neck and shoulders.

They reached a ridge. "I think we're starting to head down on the Wilburn side of the mountain," she said to Nugget, as if he understood what she was saying. Now they seemed to be heading mostly downhill, The trail was pretty rocky here so the going was slow. As they rounded a bend, Bailey could see a straight section and picked up a trot again. There were some rocks, but Nugget picked his way through them pretty well. They had gone a distance when Bailey spotted the pine grove. "At last!" she almost shouted.

Bailey turned Nugget onto the right-hand trail and continued trotting. It started getting quite rocky again, and she slowed Nugget to a walk. After that the trail flattened out and they were able to trot again. Suddenly, Bailey could see a house. The trail widened and she asked Nugget to pick up a lope. When they arrived at the house, Bailey dismounted, took off Nugget's bridle and let him munch on the grass.

"Mrs. Collins, hello," Bailey called out. "Anyone home? I need your help!" hollered Bailey, as she ran around to the back of the house. She saw someone bent over in the garden. "Hello, Mrs. Collins, I'm Bailey Mathews." Bailey said, almost out of breath. "A tree fell on my grandpa, Ben Slater, he's hurt and I need to get medical help for him. Can I use your phone? Our phone and satellite are out."

"Oh dear," said Sarah. "My son, Brian, is logging way over in the valley, but my grandson, Noah, isn't too far from here fixing up a storage shed. He has a cell phone with him. We don't have a phone here at the house."

"There was a rock slide blocking the mountain road, and I couldn't get through to use the Anderson's phone," Bailey explained.

"To get to where Noah is, you can take the Ridge Road, but the quickest way to get there is to go through the old mine," Sarah explained. "It's dark and a little scary, but it will save a lot of time. We use it quite often. Head right down this path, keep following it through right and left bends, it will take you right to the mine. You will see the entrance, go right in. Always keep to the right. Whenever there is a turn, keep to the right. It will bring you out on Ridge Road. Turn right on Ridge Road and follow it down till you see a shed on the right. That's the shed Noah is working on. This way is much shorter than the long loop you would have to take on Ridge Road — the mine cuts right through the mountain.

"Here, dear, take this," said Sarah, handing Bailey a flashlight. "It does get pretty dark in there. You'd better get going, Bailey."

"Thanks so much, Mrs. Collins," Bailey said, as she put the flashlight in her saddle bag. She mounted up and headed down the path.

"Tell Noah I'll see him later," Sarah called out.

Bailey followed the bends in the path and arrived at the mine. She and Nugget stood gazing into the entrance, it looked dark inside. Bailey urged Nugget forward, he stopped and looked wide-eyed. She squeezed her legs again, and he did not want to walk forward. Nugget moved sideways to the left. Bailey moved him back to the center of the opening. When he looked inside and shifted his weight forward, Bailey released the reins and her leg pressure. When he relaxed and lowered his head, she rubbed his neck. Nugget moved sideways to the right. Bailey moved him back to the center again. When he looked inside the mine and took a step forward, she released the reins and her leg pressure. This was repeated quite a few times until Nugget really relaxed and was able to walk into the mine.

Bailey turned on the flashlight as they got further into the mine. She knew that Nugget could see just fine, but she wanted to see. It smelled very musty in the tunnel. She felt Nugget's energy come up, he almost felt fizzy underneath her. Suddenly a rock fell and echoed which caused Nugget to spook and jump sideways. All this made Bailey drop the flashlight which clanged and echoed and made Nugget spook again, especially since he was already on edge. Bailey had Nugget do a few one-rein stops, disengaged his hindquarters and changed directions several more times to help him calm himself.

Once Nugget had come to a stop and was calm Bailey dismounted so she could get the flashlight.

She led Nugget back to pick up the light. As they were walking, Bailey's left foot slipped on the uneven footing and went into a hole. "Ow ow ow!" Bailey screamed as her foot twisted and landed on its side at the bottom of the hole. "Ow, that hurts," she repeated. The hole wasn't too deep, just deep enough for her ankle to twist and do some damage.

Bailey pulled her foot out, her ankle was hurting badly inside her boot. She rotated her foot slowly to see if she could move it. "Thank you, God," she said. "I don't think it's broken, I can move it." She rubbed her ankle through the boot. "I'm afraid to take my boot off," she said to Nugget. "If it swells, I might not be able to get my boot back on," she told him.

"Nugget, you're really going to have to help me now," she said almost in tears. "I think my ankle is sprained so I can't really walk on it and we have to find Noah to make that call."

Mustering all her courage, she managed to stand and get the flashlight. Bailey aimed the light around and looked for something to stand on so she could remount. She found a pile of rocks that looked promising. Bailey led Nugget to the rocks, keeping most of her weight on her right foot. She tried to wiggle the rocks with her hands, and couldn't. They seemed pretty solid. Bailey carefully climbed up on one rock, then on the next higher rock. She put the flashlight in her saddle bag.

"Okay, Nugget, pick me up," Bailey said, as she eased Nugget closer to the rocks. "I know this isn't how we usually do it," she said softly, mounting on the off side so she could use her right foot. "That's it, good boy," Bailey said, gently sitting down in the saddle. She didn't even try putting her left foot in the stirrup, she just let it hang loose.

"Let's go boy, I really want to get out of this mine," she said honestly, as they walked off.

Bailey reached in the bag and retrieved the flashlight. They continued on and passed several turns, but stayed to the right. Bailey literally spotted the "light at the end of the tunnel."

"Nugget, we made it!" she exclaimed, relieved when they emerged from the mine. Even Nugget let out a big sigh as the adrenaline totally left his body.

Chapter Four

Bailey and Nugget rode right on Ridge Road. The footing was good. Bailey was able to wriggle her left boot into the stirrup and they loped for a distance. She saw the shed and someone working there.

"Noah, Noah," she cried out. "Hi, I'm Bailey Mathews, can I use your phone?" she continued. "Your grandmother sent me to find you. My grandpa is hurt, our phones are out because of the storm, the Mountain Road is blocked by a rock slide, and I have to get help for him, his leg is broken," she blurted out all this at once, as she dismounted from the off side.

"Sure thing," Noah responded, handing her his phone.

"Thanks," Bailey said as she hobbled toward Noah. She quickly called her friend Charlie and repeated exactly what she had just told Noah. "Please tell your mom they're going to need a road crew to clear the rock slide to get the ambulance through," she added. "I had to ride all the way over to Mrs. Collins's house to call you. I'll make my way home, but it'll take me a while. Can you go check on Grandpa as soon as you can get through? He's all alone."

Bailey paused for a moment listening to Charlie's response. "Thanks, Charlie, tell Grandpa I'm okay," Bailey said. "Please call us when they can get in to help him. I'll hand the phone to Noah so he can give you his number. Thanks so much," Bailey said handing Noah back his phone, "and, thank you, God," she added, looking up for a moment. She was so relieved that she was finally able to make a call to get help for her grandpa.

Noah gave Charlie his number and watched Bailey limp around as she removed her horse's bridle and loosened his girth. "What happened to your leg?" Noah asked.

"My foot slipped while we were walking in the mine, and slid into a hole," Bailey grimaced. "I think my ankle is sprained."

"There's a creek right there. Let's get your foot into some cold water," Noah suggested. "That might help keep it from swelling too much."

"Great idea," Bailey agreed, leaving Nugget there to graze.

Noah helped Bailey walk to the creek. Bailey

pulled off her boot and sock to take a look. "It doesn't look too swollen, but it sure is sore" she said almost surprised, as she gently rubbed her ankle.

They sat for bit talking while Bailey soothed her aching ankle in the cold mountain water. "By the way, I'm Bailey Mathews. My grandpa is Ben Slater. We live on the other side of the mountain," Bailey told Noah.

"Your mom's Annie, right, the one who trains all the horses?" Noah asked. "I met her and your grandpa some years ago. Grandma knows your family, but I've never met you before."

"Yes, that's my mom. I know I've heard a lot about your family too," Bailey said as she filled in some of the details of the day.

"Well, I guess it's time we headed back," Noah suggested.

"Yes, I want to make sure Grandpa is being taken care of," Bailey said, as she rinsed her hands and took a nice long drink from the creek.

"I'm going with you," Noah stated. "I want to make sure you get home safely. With that sprained ankle, you could run into some serious trouble."

"Oh, Noah, would you?" Bailey smiled. "That would be super! The ride over here was pretty difficult in a few places. I'd feel so much better having you with me," said Bailey, feeling extremely happy and relieved.

"I'm glad to. People look out for each other in the back country," Noah smiled back at her.

Bailey gently put her sock back on, then she opened up the lacing on her boot extra wide and eased it on over the sock. "It feels really tight," she said to Noah.

"Leave it loose, don't tie it tightly," Noah suggested.

"Okay, sounds good," agreed Bailey.

They made it over to the horses. Bailey tightened Nugget's girth and put his bridle back on over his get-down rope. She found a stump and again mounted Nugget from the off side. Bailey experimented with her left foot and found it was more comfortable to leave it out of the stirrup.

Noah quickly put away some equipment and supplies from his work on the shed. He tightened his horse's girth, put a bridle on over a get-down rope and mounted up.

"Let's give them a drink first," suggested Bailey as she and Nugget headed for the creek. She noticed that Noah rode with similar tack.

Noah had dark brown hair, a nice smile and an easy way about him. Bailey thought he was about her age, maybe a year older.

"Okay, I'm right behind you," Noah called out.

The horses drank thirstily. They swished their heads in the water and took long slurps. Bailey and

Noah started up the road side-by-side toward the mine.

"He's a really nice horse," Bailey commented on the dark brown horse with a white blaze as they rode along. "Is he a quarter horse?"

"Yes, this is Gus, he's ten years old," replied Noah.

"Nugget was pretty high energy in the tunnel," Bailey warned.

"When we get to the mine, I'll lead," suggested Noah. "We'll use the power of the herd. Gus has been through the mine a lot. He'll stay calm and following him will help give Nugget some confidence."

"Good thinking, I've been studying herd dynamics," Bailey interjected. She pulled out the flashlight and they entered the mine. "Well, that's how I met Nugget. There's a herd of wild mustangs that travels through a far section of the mountain, and I've been documenting them for a school project."

"Wait, Nugget's a wild mustang?" Noah asked in surprise.

"Yes," Bailey assured him. "He started approaching me and my horse Moses after we had been observing them everyday for months in one of the fields."

"That's amazing!" Noah exclaimed. "It seems so unlikely that anything like that would happen."

Bailey wished she could've seen the look on Noah's face, but it was dark and she and Nugget were following him.

"Nugget seems way more calm following Gus," Bailey said happily.

"He's doing great," Noah agreed. "So tell me more. How did you catch him?"

"I didn't catch him, it's more like he caught us," Bailey laughed. "Over time, he started investigating Moses and me. Moses is my older broke saddle horse. Nugget would come closer and closer, then suddenly there he was grazing along side Moses. The three of us became really good friends. I started working and playing with him and one day, I ponied him home."

"What a story!" Noah said excitedly. "You've got a real gift with horses, like your mom."

"Thanks, that's what my mom tells me, but I feel like I have so much to learn," Bailey admitted.

"We all have a lot to learn," said Noah in a reassuring way.

Bailey found herself thinking, "Noah's so easy to talk to. I just met him, but I feel like I've known him my whole life!"

"Why didn't you ride Moses today?" Noah asked.

"He's got some swelling in his left front leg. I iced it, but I wouldn't take a chance on riding him and making it worse," replied Bailey.

In no time, they were out of the mine heading toward Noah's house.

"Gus was really great going through the mine," Bailey commented.

"The first time I took him through the tunnel, he was way worse than how you described Nugget," Noah rolled his eyes. "I didn't think I was going to make it out alive!"

"What did you do to help him?" asked Bailey.

"I took him back to the closest entrance, and worked him outside the mine. Then asked him to enter. As long as he looked or moved forward calmly, that was his rest. The second he got upset, tried to back or refused to go forward, I took him out and worked him. So, being outside of the mine was work and inside was rest." Noah explained.

"Oh, you made the right thing easy and the wrong thing difficult," Bailey smiled.

"Exactly!" Noah smiled back. "After a while he wasn't so eager to be out of the mine."

They arrived at the house and Sarah came out. "Were you able to arrange for help, dear?" asked Sarah.

"Yes, my friend Charlie said she will call when they get to Grandpa." Bailey answered, as she dismounted from the off side. She made her way over to the front steps and sat down.

"I'm so glad," said Sarah.

"Grandma, I'm getting a cold pack for Bailey's ankle," said Noah. "She sprained it in the mine." Noah dismounted, then loosened the horses' girths and took off their bridles.

"They're in the freezer," offered Sarah.

"Here Bailey," Noah said, reaching his hand out a few minutes later, giving Bailey the cold pack.

"Thanks, Noah," Bailey said, pulling off her boot and putting the cold pack on her ankle.

"How's your ankle feeling?" Noah said as he sat on the step next to Bailey.

"It's pretty sore, she said.

"Grandma, I'm going with Bailey to make sure she gets home safely," Noah said firmly.

"That's a very good idea, Noah," Sarah said. "She still has a long way to go."

"If you come with me, better ride a horse that likes to jump," Bailey said to Noah with a chuckle. "There's a huge tree down across the trail. Nugget and I had to jump it and I'm not sure I can do it now with this ankle."

"I'll pack a chain saw and some ropes," Noah suggested. "With some luck I'll be able to clear the trail."

Sarah came back out with a couple sandwiches. "You two better eat something before you head to the Slater Farm," she said.

"I don't know how to thank you both for all your help," Bailey said with a quiver in her voice.

"Just come back and visit when you feel better, Bailey," Sarah gave her a hug.

Bailey and Noah finished the sandwiches and washed them down with the water Sarah brought them. Noah fetched a chain saw, tools and ropes, and packed everything securely. They readied the horses and mounted up.

"Dad should be home about the time we get to the Slater's. I'll call him to let you both know we got there okay," Noah called out as they headed up the trail.

"Be safe," Sarah called back.

"Do you want to trot a little?" Noah asked as they started out.

"Let's lope while we can," Bailey suggested. "Most of the way we'll have to walk." She smiled and loped off with her left foot hanging free.

"All right!" Noah called out and loped off too.

They loped part of the way up the hill on Ridge Road and then broke to a trot when the footing became uneven. They had to start walking long before they reached the pine grove and turned left.

"Do you go to a regular school, Noah?" Bailey asked.

"I was home schooled for the first few years,"

Noah explained. Then I lived with my mom in town, in Wilburn, and went to regular school for a few years. Now I work part-time with my dad and live and work on the farm, so I'm in a home school program again."

"I really like being home schooled," admitted Bailey. It's more flexible. I can choose my projects, work with horses with my mom, and help on the farm."

"I do miss having more friends my age to hang out with," said Noah.

"Me too," agreed Bailey. "My friend Charlie lives a few miles down the road, we see each other as much as we can. We go to church almost every Sunday in Linville and I get to spend time with my friends there too. Our church has a potluck afterwards and youth group activities, so it's a lot of fun."

"You're lucky, that does sound like fun," Noah said, sounding a little envious.

"Speaking of friends, it looks like Nugget and Gus are becoming good friends," Bailey chuckled.

"They do seem to get along well together," Noah agreed.

"Are your parents divorced?" asked Bailey. "That's got to be hard."

"Yeah, but you get used to it after a while," Noah said with resignation.

Bailey and Noah had to go single file here as the trail got narrow and rocky.

"I'll go first," Noah offered.

"What's your favorite thing about being with horses?" asked Bailey, speaking louder now.

"Hmmm, I don't know that I've ever thought about them that way. I'm so used to having horses in my life. I love riding and trying to figure out ways to do different chores with them," Noah related. "How about you, what's your favorite thing about them?"

"I love how willing horses are to change when we change," Bailey revealed.

"You think differently from everyone I've ever known," Noah said with a lightness in his voice.

"I'm weird, huh?" Bailey smiled.

"Weird in a good way," chuckled Noah, "in a very good way."

Bailey and Noah were now mostly going downhill. Bailey noticed how Nugget wanted to be right up close to Gus's tail. She asked Nugget to slow, so that he dropped back and there was more space between the two horses. She positioned the reins on his neck. After a few strides, Nugget would speed up a little to catch up to Gus. Bailey would have a feel on the reins and lift them to ask him to slow. If he didn't slow she took up more on the reins and asked him to slow again. This went on for quite a while, she slowed him again and released pressure on the reins. Nugget let out a big sigh and just decided to stay a horse length of space behind Gus.

"Yes!" Bailey said just above a whisper. "That worked really well."

"I noticed what you were doing," Noah chimed in. "Don't you love it when a horse gets what you're after?"

"You mean when our idea becomes their idea?" queried Bailey.

"Exactly," replied Noah.

They arrived at the big tree. "You weren't lyin', it's huge!" Noah exclaimed, laughing. "You and Nugget jumped that? I'm impressed!" he kidded Bailey.

"Yes, we flew!" Bailey retorted with a smile.

"Whew!" Noah remarked as he looked up and down, and side-to-side. "Let me see what I can do here."

Noah dismounted and unpacked the chain saw and tools that were lashed onto Gus's saddle. He hopped back on and rode Gus back down the trail a distance from the tree and dismounted. Bailey followed on Nugget. "You stay with the horses," he said to Bailey.

"Sure," she said and dismounted.

"I think I can cut a section wide enough for us to get through where the trunk is narrower and the branches start. The smaller chain saw I brought just can't handle the widest part of the trunk," Noah said as he walked back to the tree.

Noah started up the chain saw and went to work. Gus wasn't bothered at all by the noise. Nugget was a little upset by the commotion, it was good they were well away. Bailey moved him around on the ground a bit. She moved him in continuous half circles, asking him to turn on each end, stop, then move in the opposite direction. Occasionally she asked him to stop and faced him toward the chain saw. She kept this up until he settled down. Nugget relaxed and dropped his head. Bailey loved the look a horse gets when it realizes it doesn't have to be afraid. "Good boy," she told Nugget.

Noah cut for a while, then turned the chainsaw off. He walked Gus over to the tree and tied one end of the rope to the saddle horn and the other end to a large branch. He mounted up and dragged the branch out of the way. Noah repeated this procedure until he had cleared a section wide enough for them to go through single file.

"That should do it," Noah yelled out, securing the rope and chainsaw back onto Gus's saddle.

"Great job," Bailey yelled back, mounting up.

"Let's head out," said Noah as Bailey and Nugget came up along-side.

"I would've had a really tough time jumping that now," Bailey admitted. "Don't think I could've made it. Guess I'll have to practice jumping with Nugget under better circumstances," she added.

Right then, Noah's phone rang. "Hello, sure," said Noah as he handed the phone to Bailey.

"Hey," Bailey said, and paused. "Great news!" Bailey exclaimed. "Call back when they get to Grandpa. Did you get my mom?" again she paused. "Cool, thanks. It'll be a while yet before we get to the farm. Talk to you soon," Bailey said, handing the phone back to Noah.

"So what's happening?" asked Noah.

"They've almost got the road cleared enough to get the ambulance through," Bailey smiled. "Mom's wrapping up the clinic, then heading home. We'll probably get to my house right about when the paramedics are helping Grandpa."

"Fantastic, let's go," said Noah, starting through the cleared section of the tree.

"Nugget, my friend, you are going to sleep tonight," Bailey laughed.

Bailey and Noah rode now on one of the prettiest parts of the trail. They traveled at an easy pace and here were able to walk side-by-side. As they rode, Bailey and Noah talked about horses and plans for the rest of the summer. They turned right onto the section of trail that followed the creek.

"This limb came down and almost clobbered Nugget and me on the way over to your house. It fell right behind us," Bailey said, pointing at the culprit. "Nugget just about jumped out of his skin and did a 360!"

"I'm so glad you didn't get clobbered," Noah said gratefully with a smile. "Whew, you were lucky! You both might have gotten hurt really badly."

"I thank God for taking care of us," sighed Bailey.

They continued on and finally reached the Mountain Road.

"A lot of dust has been kicked up, a vehicle has just come by here," Bailey said excitedly, as they turned onto the road.

"Let's hurry," Noah called out, easing into a trot, then a lope.

"Hey, wait for me!" Bailey called out, asking Nugget for a lope.

Chapter Five

As they rode into the farm, they could see the ambulance. Bailey and Noah rode up, Bailey dismounted and quickly took off Nugget's bridle. As she limped over, they were loading her grandpa into the ambulance on a stretcher.

"Grandpa, how are you feeling?" she asked, almost out of breath. "Mom's on her way home, but it'll be a few hours before she gets here," she said climbing into the ambulance and grabbing her grandpa's hand.

"Animals," he said barely audible, squeezing her hand.

"Okay, Grandpa, I'll take care of the animals," Bailey said, realizing that they hadn't been fed and no work had been done so far today.

Ben nodded and closed his eyes.

"I'll get Mom or Charlie's mom to take me to see

you as soon as I can," Bailey said, almost in tears.

"He's exhausted," said the paramedic. "We just gave him something for the pain."

"Love you, Grandpa," she said, and then stepped out of the ambulance.

Noah had untacked both horses and they were grazing on the grass.

"You're not going to the hospital?" Noah asked.

"No, I completely forgot that the animals haven't been fed or watered or anything yet today," Bailey said, feeling a little exhausted herself.

"I'll help you," Noah offered.

"You've already done so much to help me, really, both me and Grandpa today," Bailey said. "...And you have a long ride home."

Charlie and her mom, Beth, were standing nearby. "We'll help too." they said, almost at the same time.

"If we all pitch in we'll be done in no time," Beth said. "Try not to worry Bailey, your grandpa's going to be fine."

"Bailey, tell us what we need to do," said Noah. "I'm calling my dad right now to let him know we got here safely and I'm going to stay and give you a hand."

"Both the sheep and the cattle, out in the pasture, need to have their water checked and filled – the same with the pasture horses." Bailey explained.

"The horses in paddocks need hay, water and to have their manure picked up. I'll take care of the three stalled horses and Moses' leg will need icing." Bailey directed them as well as any general. "Charlie will help you find everything, she's helped me before."

"Bailey, you take it easy and ice your ankle," Noah insisted, pointing for her to sit on a hay bale. "We'll take care of everything."

"I'll get Bailey a cold pack and one for Moses' leg, too," Charlie said, heading for the house.

Within a couple hours Beth, Charlie and Noah had the chores finished. They were sitting down, drinking some water and relaxing for a moment when Annie and Ross drove in, pulling their horses in the trailer.

"Bailey, are you all right?" Annie called out as she came running over to where they were sitting. "I was so worried about you when Beth called me," she said, hugging Bailey. "Where's Grandpa?"

"They got the ambulance in and took him to the hospital a couple hours ago." Bailey said, looking worried. "I wanted to go with him, but he told me to stay and take care of the animals. I sprained my ankle, so I've got a cold pack on it.

"Mom, Ross, this is Noah Collins, Sarah's grandson," said Bailey. "He helped me get home safely. It was his phone that I used to call Charlie."

"Thank you, Noah," said Annie shaking his hand, then giving him a hug. "Thank you for helping my daughter and my dad."

"Everyone helped get the chores done, so we can go see how Grandpa's doing," Bailey explained.

"Thanks for all your help," Annie said gratefully, looking into all their faces. "How did you sprain your ankle?" Annie asked Bailey.

"I sprained it in the mine," answered Bailey. "It's a long story, I'll tell you later."

"Honey, I think you should just take it easy and keep ice on your ankle. You can see Grandpa soon," Annie suggested. "Beth, would you drive me into town to check on Dad? I'm pretty tired from the drive back home from Baxter, and I want to call Will on the way, to fill him in."

"Sure, Annie," Beth said. "We'll drop Charlie at home on the way."

"Noah, you should stay the night, it's almost dark already," Annie said, looking at her watch. "It's too dangerous to make the ride back now. Call your family and tell them you'll head back first thing in the morning. You can sleep in the old bunk house. Put your horse in a paddock or stall, whichever is better for him.

"Let's get the horses out of the trailer, so we can

get going," Annie said to Beth.

"Are you two okay with making yourselves some sandwiches for supper?" Annie said to Bailey and Noah.

"Sure, Mom," Bailey said with a chuckle. "After what we've been through today, we can easily make a couple sandwiches."

"I'm so proud of you, Bailey," Annie said, smiling and giving Bailey another squeeze. "I want to hear all about your ride to the Collins's house when I get back. I'll feel so much better when I know how your grandpa's doing," she said on her way to the trailer.

Annie and Ross got the horses settled, then Annie left in Beth's truck.

"I'm going to check on all the animals, Ross said, "then I'll come in and fix myself something to eat."

"Well, this has been quite a day," Noah said, after he had called his dad to let him know he was staying the night and going home in the morning. "My dad thought it was a good idea to go home in the morning," he added.

"I'm going to ice my ankle and elevate my foot like Mom told me," Bailey said. "Mom said to do that off-and-on for at least the first 24 hours, then soak my ankle in warm water and Epsom salt — that will be soothing tomorrow."

"How's it feeling?" Noah asked.

"It's sore and swollen, but I'm sure it will heal just fine," Bailey answered. "Let's make some sandwiches, I'm starved."

"You can sit and ice your foot while I fix the sandwiches," Noah suggested, helping Bailey into the house and to the kitchen table. "The best thing you can do to help your ankle heal, is to stay off it."

"Okay, Doc," Bailey chuckled.

"All right smarty, what do we have for sandwiches?" asked Noah, opening the refrigerator door.

"I think there's some sliced turkey left and cheeses are in the drawer," said Bailey. "Mustard and mayo are on the door, lettuce and tomatoes are in the bin, and oh, don't forget the pickles. They're in there somewhere."

"Great, where's the bread?" Noah asked, piling the items on the table.

"In the cupboard, there," Bailey pointed. "Knives and forks are in that drawer and we can use paper towels for plates, less dishes to wash," she laughed. "The cutting board is there," she pointed again.

"How's this? We can each make our own the way we like it," Noah smiled, handing Bailey a knife and a couple sheets of paper towel. "I'll slice some tomatoes."

"Hand me some pepper jack cheese please, yum,

that's my favorite," said Bailey, stretching out her hand. Bailey was thinking how cute Noah looked when he smiled.

"Here you go." Noah smiled again.

"How long does it take for a sprained ankle to heal?" asked Bailey.

"At least a few days, maybe a week or more," said Noah.

"What can I do sitting around for that long?" thought Bailey out loud. "I can work on my home school projects and if Mom sets up saddles and bridles, I can clean and oil tack. I guess, I'll be able to help out a little. I can watch Mom train horses and take notes. That is if she has time to train horses, she and Ross have all the chores to do with Grandpa hurt and me off my feet. Dad will be home next week, but that won't help this week."

"I can come and help with chores a couple days," offered Noah. I can't come every day because I have chores and work to do at home."

"I know Mom would appreciate anything you could do," Bailey said gratefully. "You've already done so much to help us, I hate for you to do more."

"That's okay," Noah said. "I'd really like to watch your mom work horses. If I come help out, maybe I'll get a chance to do that. I want to learn more."

"I'm sure Mom would be happy to have you watch," Bailey commented. She's currently starting a couple three-year-old quarter horses."

"Cool, that would be great!" Noah exclaimed.

"What are you studying in your school projects?" asked Bailey.

"I'm studying forestry, natural resources and wildlife management," Noah answered. "It's really interesting and it ties in with my dad's logging business, but I love working with horses, too. How about you, what are you studying?" he asked.

"Equine studies, agriculture and farming," answered Bailey. "I love it all. Your study areas sound fascinating too. Sometimes I wish I had a brain as big as a house so I could fit in more stuff."

"What a great thought!" Noah said laughing. "Now we just have to figure out how to create bigger brains...or invent a way to compress the information so we can fit more into our current sized brains!" He made a face and gestured like his head was about to explode.

"That's a great idea too!" said Bailey, while they were both laughing. "The way things are progressing, soon all of us will be directly connected via Wi-Fi, able to access huge amounts of information through computers and the internet. We won't need to store it all in our own brains."

"Problem solved," Noah agreed, laughing.

They were both still laughing when they heard a truck pull in.

"Grandpa's leg is broken and he has a pretty bad concussion," Annie explained. They are keeping him to do more tests to see if he has any internal injuries and to monitor the concussion. He'll be there at least until tomorrow and maybe longer, but they said he should be fine. I'm going to call later to see if they have any other information."

"I'm so glad he's going to be okay, Mom, and that he's getting good care," sighed Bailey, feeling relieved and suddenly feeling really tired."

"Honey, you look really beat. You should get some sleep," Annie said, rubbing Bailey's shoulder.

"Noah, there are some sheets, blankets and pillows in the hall closet upstairs. Grab what you need. I'll get you a flashlight. The bunk house is to the right of the barn. The light switch is just inside the door. You can make up your bed, right?" Annie asked.

"Sure, Mrs. Mathews, I'll be fine," answered Noah.

I double checked all the animals," Ross said, as he came in the door, "they're all good for the night."

"Ross, can you find the crutches from when you had a broken leg?" Annie asked. "Your sister needs to use them. Then help Noah and make sure he can find everything he needs."

"I think the crutches are in the attic, I'll get them," Ross replied, "come on, Noah."

"Now, let me take a look at your ankle," Annie said, squatting down. "Yes, you have quite a sprain here sweetie. When we go see Grandpa tomorrow, let's get it checked out just to be sure it's not more serious."

"Okay, Mom," agreed Bailey.

The boys came back carrying all the bedding and the crutches. "Good, Ross, get Noah settled into the bunk house, and I'll help Bailey get to bed," Annie said. "I think we all need a good night's sleep."

"Can you manage with these for tonight?" asked Annie. "We can adjust them tomorrow."

"The stairs will be the trickiest part," Bailey said.

"I'll be right with you, just in case," Annie said, as they headed for the stairs.

Annie had helped Bailey into bed when Ross popped his head in the bedroom door. "Noah's all settled into the bunk house, Mom, and I just grabbed a sandwich," Ross said. "I'm hitting my pillow. It's going to be a busy day tomorrow. Glad you're okay, Sis," Ross nodded at Bailey.

"Thanks Ross, see you in the morning," replied Annie.

"Thanks, Ross," Bailey echoed.

Bailey's eyelids felt like they weighed a ton. She started to tell her mom about everything that had

happened, but her mom noticed her drooping eyelids and said, "Sleep now, you can tell me all about it
in the morning."

"Goodnight, Mom," Bailey said sleepily.

Annie gave Bailey a hug and said, "I'm so glad
you are safe, sweetie." She kissed the top of Bailey's
head, and turned out the light.

"Good morning, Mrs. Mathews," Noah said
cheerily, as he entered the kitchen. "What can I do
before I head home?" he asked.

"First, you can sit down and have some breakfast,"
Annie replied.

Ross came in and sat down. "Morning everyone,"
he said, as he poured some juice.

"If you boys could do the morning chores, that
would be a huge help," Annie said, as she placed
plates of scrambled eggs, bacon and toast in front of
them. "Bailey and I are going to see how Grandpa's
doing and get her ankle checked while we're there."

"You got it, Mom," said Ross.

"Then I want you to leave for home, Noah," said
Annie. "I appreciate all you've done to help us, but
I'm sure your family needs you too. You'll be okay
for the ride home won't you?"

"I'll be fine, Mrs. Mathews," Noah replied. I'd like

to come back day after tomorrow to help out, if it's okay with my dad. Bailey told me that you're starting some three year olds and I'd really like the chance to watch."

"Only if it's okay with your dad," Annie agreed. "We could certainly use the extra help with Grandpa and Bailey off their feet and my husband away till next week. You're very welcome to watch me work the horses," Annie added.

"That would be great," Noah said.

Bailey came in using the crutches. "Morning everyone," she said, leaning the crutches and sitting down. "Smells good."

"How's your ankle feeling this morning?" Noah asked Bailey.

"It's still sore, but it's feeling a little better, thanks," Bailey replied.

"The boys are going to do the morning chores, then Noah's riding home. You and I are going into town shortly to see how Grandpa's doing and have your ankle checked," Annie said, placing a breakfast plate in front of Bailey.

"Thanks, Mom," Bailey said, digging in. "My ankle doesn't look so swollen."

"I know dear, but I'd feel better if we get it checked," Annie insisted. "I want to be sure."

"Sure, Mom, you're right," Bailey agreed.

"Let's put a cold pack on your ankle again before

we leave," Annie said.

"Come on, Noah," Ross said, finishing his last gulp of eggs and getting up from the table. "Let's get those chores done."

"I'll be back on Tuesday, Bailey," Noah said, following Ross. "See you then."

"Okay, thanks again for all your help, Noah," Bailey called after him as he went out the door.

Chapter Six

"So tell me everything that happened, honey," Annie said, on the drive into town.

Bailey related all the events since right before the storm, only leaving out some of her personal feelings about Noah. She wasn't ready to share those feelings with anyone yet.

"Oh, Grandpa," Bailey sighed, close to tears, when she hugged him. "I was so worried about you. How are you feeling?"

"I'm hurting some," said Ben, trying not to show it too much. "I don't know how long they're going to keep me here yet."

"I'm going to talk to the doctor and see what he says," Annie said. "Did they do any tests this morning?"

"Not yet. They said they were coming back shortly to do another test," Ben said, grumbling a bit.

"They kept me up half the night. I only got a couple hours sleep."

"I'll see what I can find out," Annie said as she left the room.

"We took care of all the animals. Beth, Charlie and Noah did all the work last night." Bailey told Grandpa. "Then this morning Noah and Ross did the chores. They wouldn't let me help, but made me ice my sprained ankle."

Annie came back in. "They're taking you in a few minutes to run another test." Annie explained. "If it looks good, they may release you to go home."

"That would be great," said Ben.

"Since you're going to be here a while longer, Dad, I'm going to take Bailey downstairs to get her ankle checked — just to be sure. We'll be back in a little while."

"Sounds like a good idea," Ben agreed.

"Good news, Dad," Annie said, walking back into Ben's room. "Bailey's ankle is just sprained, no other issues. If she keeps weight off it, alternates icing it and soaking it in warm water and Epsom salt, it should feel better in a week."

"I'm really glad to hear that," said Ben.

"Did they give you that test yet?" asked Annie,

pouring Ben some water from the pitcher on the table next to his bed.

"Yes, but I haven't heard anything since," said Ben.

"I'll go check with the nurse," Annie said, heading back toward the door.

"Mom, I'm going to stay with Grandpa for a while," Bailey said, sitting in the chair next to her grandpa.

"I'll be back in a few minutes," Annie said, her voice trailing off into the hall.

"I'm so glad you're okay. Grandpa," Bailey said hugging him. "I didn't want to leave you – I was so worried about you."

"I know, sweetheart," said Ben hugging her back. "I needed you to make that ride to get help for me. You stepped up to the plate and you really came through. I'm so proud of you."

"I'd do anything for you," Bailey said.

"I'd do anything for you too," Ben said. "That's what families do."

"I wouldn't have been able to do it without Noah's help. He's coming back to help out with chores day after tomorrow," Bailey said. "He also wants to watch Mom work with the two horses she's starting under saddle."

"He certainly seems like a nice young man," Ben added. "I hope you thanked him for all he did to help us."

"Oh, of course," Bailey said. "Mom thanked him too and she gave him a big hug."

"You know, his grandma and grandpa and I go way back," Ben said. "We were the first two families up on the mountain. Walt, his grandpa, and I were good friends. We saved each other's bacon more than once. Walt's been gone a few years now."

"I'd love to hear about those times Grandpa," Bailey said. "Will you tell me some of those stories?"

"I sure will honey, but first I want to hear all about your ride over to Sarah's place," Ben said.

Bailey recounted all the events of her journey the previous day. She and Ben were still laughing about when she and Nugget practically jumped out their skins when the big bough came down, when Annie walked back into the room.

"Glad to see you laughing Dad," Annie smiled.

"We were laughing about when Bailey and Nugget jumped out of their skins when the big branch came down," Ben said.

"Bailey had quite a day yesterday, didn't she?" Annie commented.

"She sure did," Ben replied. "Bailey really came through when the chips were down. She showed real courage and skill."

"Yes, she did. We should have a cookout after you get home to thank everyone who helped us out," Annie said. "Speaking of after you get home, Dr.

Ames wants to keep you overnight one more night. He said you have a pretty bad concussion and they want to monitor you for a little longer to make sure. He also said with your broken leg it will help you to have more care for at least one more day. He'll be in to talk to you shortly."

"That's kind of what I thought he would say." said Ben. "It took a lot out of me. Honestly, I can use the bed rest. If I could get some sleep, that would help."

"I know, Dad," said Annie, leaning over to kiss him. "We're going. I have a lot to do and maybe you can get some sleep. We'll be back tomorrow to pick you up and take you home."

"Grandpa looks so much better," said Bailey, on the way to the truck. "Can we stop and get an ice cream to eat on the way home?"

"Yes, we can use a treat," Annie answered. "What are you going to get?"

"I'm getting black angus with extra hot fudge, in a cup," said Bailey.

"What's black angus?" asked Annie.

"It's black raspberry with dark chocolate chunks," answered Bailey.

"Hmmm...sounds delicious," said Annie. "I might get one of those too!"

"I can clean tack, if you or Ross set up some saddles for me," Bailey said as they arrived at the ranch. "I know you two have a lot to do and I want to help."

"Okay," Annie said. "Get yourself settled in the tack room and I'll get you a cold pack. We'll set up a couple saddles."

"Hey kid, how's Grandpa doing?" Ross asked as Bailey walked down the barn aisle using the crutches.

"Much better," Bailey replied. "I think he'll be coming home tomorrow."

"That's great!" Ross said happy to hear the good news.

"Will you set up a couple saddles in the tack room for me to clean and oil?"

"Sure, Sis," Ross said. "Both Mom's saddle and mine really need some TLC."

"Here's your cold pack, Bailey," Annie said, stepping into the tack room and handing it to her.

"Hey, Mom," Ross said. "Beth came by and brought food from her and friends at church. She had me put some of the containers in the freezer and some in the fridge for tonight."

"That's so nice," Annie said. "It'll be great to have meals already prepared for a couple nights. Everyone's been so helpful."

Bailey could hear her mom and Ross discussing the chores as they worked together in the barn. She busied herself cleaning the saddles. Bailey actually liked cleaning tack. She loved the smell and feel of the leather and oil. She also loved the way the saddles and other tack looked almost new after they were cleaned.

While Bailey cleaned the saddles, she thought about the ride over to the Collins's house and back the previous day, she thought about meeting Noah and she thought about her grandpa. Then she thought about Nugget and how grateful she was that they managed to get there and back in one piece. She also thought about some of the things she wanted to work on with Nugget. Bailey finished cleaning both saddles. She checked them over carefully and was satisfied with how they looked. Bailey found a notepad and pen in the tack room and made some notes about better control over the different body parts of the horse, jumping, noisy engines, spooking in place and several other things. These were things she wanted to ask her mom about and learn more ways to help Nugget, and be safe.

Suddenly, Bailey realized she was thinking about Noah again and was looking forward to seeing him tomorrow. "I hope he comes tomorrow," she almost said out loud. Bailey found the bridles that Ross and her mom used and started cleaning them.

"How's it going?" Annie said popping her head in the tack room door.

"I've finished the saddles and I'm cleaning your bridles now," Bailey replied.

"Great, we're just about ready to saddle up and check some of the pasture fencing for storm damage," Annie remarked.

"Oh, Mom, I made a list of some things I want to work on. After my ride to the Collins's place yesterday, I could sure use your help in some areas.

"Sounds like a good plan dear," Annie commented. "We'll start on them after you're all healed up."

"What else can I do to help?" Bailey asked.

"You can clean more of the tack and look for any that need repairs or you can work on your school projects," Annie replied.

"I think I'll take a break from this for now and work on my school projects," Bailey said. "I can clean more tack tomorrow. I'm going to the house now."

"Okay, sweetie. Ross and I will be in after we check the fences," Annie said.

"See you in a bit, Mom."

Bailey worked on her projects, organizing some of her data. After Ross and her mom came back, her mom heated up a lasagna that Beth brought, and they sat at the table enjoying the meal.

"We found a few places where branches came down on the fencing in the sheep pasture," Annie said. "Ross, tomorrow you can do the morning chores and set up a couple more saddles for Bailey to clean. When Noah gets here, you two can work on fixing the fencing. I'll be going into town to pick up your grandpa. After I get Grandpa settled in here, I'll try to work at least one horse. I have to keep making progress with them."

"What about the big tree that hurt Grandpa and took out the satellite dish?" asked Ross.

"We'll have to work on the tree after the damage to the fences, probably in the next couple of days," answered Annie. "Your dad will fix the satellite dish when he comes home next week, so we have some time to work on it. If we can't get to the tree, your dad will take care of it after he gets back."

"Sounds good," said Ross.

"Bailey, I want you to focus on the tack, your school work and helping out with whatever Grandpa needs, but I don't want you putting any weight on that ankle," Annie smiled at Bailey. "Okay?"

"Sure, Mom," Bailey nodded. "Can I watch when you work one of the horses and take notes?"

"Of course, sweetie," Annie answered. "That's part of your school work too."

"Sounds like a good plan," Ross commented.

"We'll all be helping Grandpa," Annie added. Whenever anyone is close to the house, we all need to check and see what he needs," Annie added. "Oh, also, when Grandpa starts feeling better, he's going want to feel useful and keep busy," Annie continued. "We'll all need to help set him up with things to do."

"Okay, Mom," Bailey and Ross said together.

"It's going to be a busy week, but we'll manage just fine if we work together. Next week, when your dad gets home, everything will be a bit easier.

"I'm going up to my room and read till bedtime," said Bailey.

"Take a cold pack with you," Annie said.

"I almost always keep one handy," Bailey chuckled, juggling the crutches while getting a cold pack out of the freezer.

The day started with a breakfast of fresh fruit, plain yogurt and toast with peanut butter. Bailey was getting better at maneuvering with the crutches. She helped her mom clean up after breakfast.

"I'm going to get the recliner all set up for Grandpa," Bailey said. "Let's see, pillow, throw, reading glasses, a couple books...anything else Mom?"

"That's good for now," Annie responded. "We'll see what else he wants when he gets home. He may just want to take a nap."

"Okay...I'm going to do some school work, then I'll work on tack," Bailey said.

"I'll see you in a while," Annie said, leaving for the hospital.

Bailey was working on her school projects when she heard a voice and knocking.

"Hello, Bailey, are you in the house?" Noah hollered out as he knocked and peeked in at the kitchen door.

"I'm in the living room," Bailey called out, as a big smile came to her face.

"Hey there, how you feeling?" Noah smiled back at her.

"So much better," Bailey replied. "It's amazing how much a good night's sleep does to make me feel better. My ankle's still sore, but it doesn't look so swollen. I'm learning how to get around easier with the crutches too."

"That's great," Noah said. "Where's Ross?" he asked. "I promised to help with the chores."

"He should be around the barn," Bailey answered. "He's doing chores while waiting for you. You and Ross are going to fix the fencing where branches came down from the storm. He and Mom found the damaged spots yesterday afternoon."

"Sounds like a plan!" Noah responded.

"After Mom gets back and gets Grandpa settled in, she's going to work some horses. She said we could watch."

"Cool," Noah smiled. "I can't wait."

"I'll be out in the tack room in a little while," Bailey smiled too. "I'm cleaning and repairing tack."

"I've figured out some ways to make repairs easier, I could show you sometime," offered Noah.

"I could definitely use some tips, Bailey added. "I'm so glad you could come." It seemed she couldn't stop smiling.

"Me too," said Noah. "My dad wanted me to do some other work on our farm, but I talked him into letting me come. I can catch up at home soon enough. See you in a while."

Bailey finished up on her schoolwork and then headed out to the tack room. She was in the tack room when her mom pulled in with Grandpa. She went to the house to help get her grandpa settled and comfortable.

"I'm so tired, I just want to go to bed," Ben said. "I didn't get much sleep in the hospital."

"Sure, Dad," Annie said, as she helped him into bed. "We'll check on you in a while, okay?"

"Thanks, honey," Ben said. "Just get me a glass of water."

"Here you are, Grandpa," Bailey said as she put the glass on the night stand. "I'm so glad you're home. Hope you get some good sleep."

Chapter Seven

"Ross and I finished fixing the storm damage to the fences," Noah told Annie as he sat down next to Bailey on the bench outside the round pen.

"Thanks so much, Noah," Annie said as she led Raina into the pen. "What's Ross doing now?"

"He's doctoring some of the sheep," Noah answered. "Some of them had scrapes from running over rocks or through brambles during the storm. Nothing looked too serious, and Ross said it didn't look like any were lost. He's doing a count."

"That's a relief," Annie sighed. "Let's get started. I'm asking Raina to move to the left at a walk. I'm asking the same things I've asked her during several previous sessions. I always start with the least amount of energy, and then I increase the energy or pressure until she does what I ask, then I immediately release the pressure."

"How does she know what you're asking?" Noah asked.

"I'm using body language and energy, backed up with the pressure of my stick and string," Annie replied. "I turn my core," she said pointing just above her abdomen, "toward whichever part of the horse I want to move. Putting my shoulders back and standing straight opens my core. Slouching a bit closes my core. Of course none of this means anything to the horse until I increase the energy or pressure by either moving toward the horse or with my stick and string. Once she figures out the lighter request comes before the increased pressure, she'll start responding sooner. Pressure directed in front of the driveline at the horse's head, neck or shoulders either stops or turns the horse, pressure behind the driveline toward the heart, abdomen or hind end either makes the horse move forward or disengages the hind end," Annie said as she turned her core and put pressure on Raina's hind end. Raina disengaged her hind end and came toward Annie as Annie backed up.

"This is so amazing," Noah commented. "I do so many things with horses and most of the time things work out pretty well, but I never knew why horses do what they do, or how I can make changes to improve my interactions with them."

"The most important thing is that you want to improve your communication skills with horses," Annie stated. "That is truly the first step to safer and better horsemanship. Horses out-weigh us, we really can't out-muscle them, we have to out-think them. The best way is to think and feel with them, have them think and feel with us – think, feel and do together."

"I'm going to shut-up now and just watch you," Noah said. "I'm talking too much and interrupting your session."

"See how my backing up drew Raina toward me," Annie said. "This is called draw. My ability to drive Raina away and draw her to me, ideally should be about even. All horses are looking for a leader to follow. The leader has the ability to move the other horse's feet. When I can move the horse's feet, without fear, calmly and with understanding, the horse wants to follow me. Raina doesn't even know why she is following me, it's instinct. All she knows is, someone is in charge – she is relaxed, safe and she feels good. She learns that being with me feels good. This is my goal. There are some conditions for this arrangement. Raina wants to be with me now, but I don't want her running me over if she does get scared. I have to protect myself by insisting on protecting my space. I create a bubble of several feet of space completely surrounding me. Raina cannot enter this space under any circumstances, unless I invite her in. I can touch her, she cannot touch me. She can approach me, but just to the edge of my bubble. This helps to keep me safe."

"This is like a college course on inter-species communication, it just blows me away!" Noah exclaimed. "I can't wait to try all of this with Gus."

"Mom makes it all look way easier than it is," Bailey commented. "It takes time to get good with the timing, body position and tools, but we'll help you."

"That would be wonderful," Noah said gratefully.

"I'm in front of Raina directing my core pressure at her head and chest, asking her to back up," explained Annie. I raise my energy and open my core, if Raina doesn't back, I press with my core energy, if she doesn't back, I add pressure with my stick pushing it toward her. She shifts her weight back, I release the pressure and relax, letting her know she did what I wanted her to do. I repeat the process. This time see she shifts her weight back when I press with my core energy. I relax and release the pressure. I do it again and Raina responds by shifting her weight back. This time, I keep pressure on when she shifts her weight back instead of releasing, and there, she takes a full step back, now I release. The horse doesn't learn from pressure, but from the release of pressure."

"I think I need to take notes," Noah said.

"Here you go," Bailey said, pulling out her pad

and pen. "You can use these," she said, handing them to Noah. "I take notes all the time," she said. "It helps me remember."

"Thanks," Noah said, smiling.

Annie repeated the same tasks as the previous sessions with Raina, explaining as she worked. "That's enough for Raina for today," Annie said, putting on the halter. "Noah would you put her in her paddock to soak and bring out Chance?"

"Sure thing, Mrs. Mathews," Noah said, reaching for Raina's lead rope.

"Which horse is progressing faster?" Noah asked as he handed Chance's lead to Annie.

"I don't really think about horses that way." Annie responded, "Each horse is so different, physically, mentally and emotionally, not to mention where they are in their training. I mostly focus on being with them in the moment, making sure they understand what it is that I'm asking of them, while keeping in mind what I think they need next. Of course, I have an overall plan for training that I follow for all the horses I work with."

"I have so much to learn," Noah said. "I need to keep watching, listening and then practicing," he said to Bailey.

Annie went through the same exercises with Chance. After that, she put the halter and lead rope on him and worked online.

"Notice that as I break things down into smaller pieces, Chance understands more quickly," Annie explained. "I ask him to put his head down by putting light pressure on his poll, and wait. If he doesn't respond, I increase the pressure. He dropped his head a bit, so I release and rub. Then I repeat this again. It helps if his head and neck are slightly bent to one side or the other. If he doesn't respond, I can add a little pressure on the lead rope to help him understand what I'm asking him to do. Most horses are very willing as long as they're not afraid and they understand your request."

"Chance seems to be getting much softer now dropping his head," Bailey commented.

"Yes, he is," agreed Annie. "If the horse is soft and relaxed, it makes it much easier for the horse to mentally understand what you want and physically do what you are asking him to do."

"That makes a lot of sense," Noah chimed in.

"Now I'm moving each part of his body, disengaging his hindquarters, then moving the front end around," Annie explained. "If I can move a part, I can control that part of the horse. I am moving the front end, then the hind end, the front end and the hind end again. I am using the fence so the horse cannot go forward. I am closing all the doors except where I want him to move, and I'm asking him to move away from pressure. Horses are naturally into pressure animals. Now I'm combining the two movements, and asking him to move sideways along the fence."

"Did I miss everything?" Ross asked as he rode up on Hondo.

"Pretty much," Bailey said. "Mom already worked Raina and I think she's finishing up with Chance."

"Shoot!" Ross said. "I really wanted to watch these sessions, but some of the sheep were scraped up pretty badly and needed doctoring."

"I'm so glad that you are studying to become a vet," Annie said. "Everyone here has to be able to doctor animals, but you are gaining so much knowledge and it sure is helpful. Now the sheep will heal well and the cuts won't get infected."

"Thanks, Mom," Ross said. "You know that's what I like to do best."

"I'm finished with Chance," Annie said. "Noah, would you put Chance in his paddock?"

"I got him," Noah said, grabbing the lead.

"Noah, you should probably head home before it gets too late," Annie suggested. "Thanks for the help with the fences."

"Okay, Mrs. Mathews," Noah said. "Glad to help. Thanks for letting me watch your training sessions. I really learned a lot."

"Anytime, Noah," Annie said.

"Noah, thanks for the help," Ross said. "It would

have taken me all day to fix the fences by myself."

"Bailey, when is the next church potluck going to be?" Noah asked. "I'd like to go."

"They are planning to have one this Sunday," Bailey replied.

"I'll have to check with my dad, but maybe I can go," Noah said.

"Okay, maybe I'll see you then," Bailey said, smiling.

"See you all soon," Noah said as he mounted up and rode off.

"Noah's such a nice young man. I have a feeling we'll be seeing him around here often," Annie commented, smiling.

"Mom, we're just friends," Bailey said, blushing, and wasn't sure she'd ever blushed before.

"We'd better check on Grandpa," Annie said. "He's probably awake by now and feeling pretty hungry."

"I'm starving!" exclaimed Ross. "We didn't stop to eat lunch today."

"I'm famished too," said Bailey, really glad the subject had changed.

Ben was awake when they came in.

"Would you like something to eat, Dad?" Annie asked.

"Yes, I'm really hungry," Ben replied, as he sat up in bed. "Boy, I was really tired. What time is it?"

"It's about three in the afternoon," Annie replied.

"We had so much to do, we didn't even stop for lunch. We're all going to have a late lunch."

"I slept a long time," Ben said. "I guess I must have needed it."

"Do you want to get up or eat here?" Annie queried.

"I'd like to get up for a while, Ben answered. "Then maybe I'll sleep tonight and really catch up on the sleep I lost."

By the time Annie had helped Ben into the kitchen, Ross and Bailey had everything laid out on the table for lunch.

"It's so good to be home," Ben said. "I sure had enough of that hospital."

"Grandpa, how are you feeling?" Bailey asked.

"Much better now that I got some sleep," Ben answered. "Hospitals are great when you need them, but it's way better when you get out of them," Ben laughed. They all laughed, as he handed his crutches to Annie and got seated in the chair.

"What do you want, Grandpa?" Bailey asked. We have potato salad and stuff for sandwiches. Beth brought over a bunch of food that friends from the church fixed for us."

"A turkey sandwich with lettuce and tomato, and some potato salad sounds terrific," Ben replied.

"Grandpa, is your leg painful?" Ross asked.

"It's not too bad," Ben replied. "The pain medication they gave me at the hospital is starting to wear off. I should probably take some more after I eat."

"That sounds like a good idea, Dad," Annie said.

"Here you are, Grandpa," Bailey said, as she put Ben's plate in front of him. "Just the way you like it, with mustard and mayo on whole wheat bread."

"I'll bring you up-to-date since the storm," Annie said. "Ross and Noah repaired fence damage this morning. Ross doctored injured sheep, and it doesn't look like we had any losses. Bailey cleaned and repaired tack. Then Bailey and Noah watched while I worked Raina and Chance. We haven't started on the monster tree yet. If Ross can't get to it, it'll be Will's job when he gets home. He will have to fix or replace the satellite dish too, so we can have the internet and TV again. Depending on how work goes, Ross may be able to start on the tree before Will gets home.

"It sounds like you've got the bases covered pretty well," said Ben.

"I'm going to be your personal gofer, Grandpa," Bailey announced. "Anything you want or need, I've got it."

"Thanks, dear," Ben said. "I appreciate it. I'm sure I'll need your help."

"I'm going out to feed," Ross said, as he got up from the table. Is there anything in particular that you want me to do, Grandpa?"

"Yes, check the hay loft," Ben said. "See if there

were any leaks in the roof from the storm. We don't want to lose any hay because of mold."

"Good thinking, Grandpa," Ross said. "It hadn't even dawned on me, I'll check it out." Ross picked up some of the empty plates and put them in the sink before going out to the barn.

"Annie, would you give me a hand to my recliner?" Ben asked. "I'd like to read for a while."

"Sure Dad," Annie replied. "It will be nice when Will gets home and we have TV and the internet again. When did the doctor say he wants you to come in to see him?"

"He said in a few weeks," Ben replied. "If I have problems, he said to call or come in sooner. The main thing he told me was, to rest, elevate my leg and don't put any weight on it."

"That sounds good," Annie said.

"As soon as you can get the most important things done," Ben said. "You've got to start haying."

"I've been concerned about that too," Annie said.

"We'll get caught up," Ben said. "We've been through tough times before."

"I know, Dad," Annie said. "It's especially hard with both you and Bailey out of commission, and Will away."

"It's a good thing we didn't have any hay cut when the storm hit," Ben added.

"That's a fact, Dad," Annie realized. "Do you think

we should hire some temporary help?"

"That might be a very good idea," Ben replied. "Let me rest a bit and think about it. I should have my head on straight soon and we can talk about it."

"It's going to take several days before you feel better. Relax for now," Annie said, as she leaned over and gave him a kiss. "I'm so glad you're home."

"Me too," said Ben. "Ask Bailey to bring me a cup of coffee, would you?"

"Sure, Dad," Annie replied. "I'm going out to help Ross with afternoon chores. Since we had a late lunch, we'll have dinner a little later than usual."

"Okay, dear," Ben said. "I'm going to mull things over a bit."

"We'll have another one of the dishes that Beth brought over with a salad," said Annie. "What a godsend these casseroles are. I'm so grateful for our friends."

"Here, Grandpa," Bailey said, as she set the mug down on the end table next to his recliner. "Can I get anything else for you?"

"Yes, would you get me a pad and pen?" Ben requested.

"I think I saw some in the drawer next to you," Bailey said, fishing around in the drawer. "Here they are!" she smiled, handing them to Ben.

"I want to jot down some ideas," Ben mumbled.

"Will you tell me those stories about you and

Noah's grandpa?" asked Bailey.

"I will sweetie," Ben said, "but not today."

"Okay, I'll be working on my mustang herd project right here," Bailey said. "Holler if you need anything."

Chapter Eight

The next day, they were all up bright and early, including Ben.

"How'd you sleep last night?" Annie asked, as she pulled out the chair at the breakfast table for Ben.

"Pretty darn good!" responded Ben. "It's amazing how a good night's sleep helps you feel so much better. I think we should hire that young fellow who helped us a few years ago when Will was working on the rig for a whole month. What was his name?"

"That's a good plan," Annie agreed. "I think his name was Lucas. He was a good worker."

"We don't want to get too far behind," said Ben. "We could miss out on hay harvesting, chance the hay getting over mature or ruined."

"You're absolutely right, Dad," Annie said smiling.

"I used your phone to check the weather," Ben said. "It looks like we have four good days straight, maybe longer."

"I'll call him," Annie said. "I should have his phone number. If not, someone at church should have it. We might get a few fields hayed before Will gets home."

"Now what about our plan for today?" Ben asked.

"We're down a man from yesterday," Ross said. "Mom, you and I should concentrate on getting the chores done."

"We wouldn't be this far along without Noah's help," Annie stated.

"That's the truth!" Ross added. "If there's time after we finish chores, Mom, you can work horses and I'll start on the monster tree."

"I like this," Annie laughed. "Ross is making the schedule!"

"Feels real good!" laughed Ross. "I could get used to this!"

"Oh, and Grandpa takes it easy and Bailey is Grandpa's personal gofer," Ross added, laughing.

"Ross the Boss!" Bailey said laughing.

"There we have it!" Ben exclaimed. "We couldn't have a better crew!"

"Grandpa and I are the rehab twins!" Bailey exclaimed. "We're getting better together."

They all had a good laugh.

"Let's get started!" Ross commanded, still laughing.

"I'll let everyone know when and if I can line Lucas up to help us," Annie said.

"I'll clean up after breakfast," Bailey said. "I can get around well enough now."

"Super, that's a big help," Annie said. "I'll be out in the barn."

"I'll be out after I do some work on my project," said Bailey. "I want you to explain something to me."

"Okay," Annie said, grabbing a second cup of coffee to take with her.

"Grandpa, I finished cleaning up and did some work on my project," Bailey stated. "Do you need anything before I go out to the barn for a while?"

"Would you fill up my coffee cup?" Ben asked.

"Here you go," Bailey said, as she poured the hot coffee. "I'll come back in shortly to see if you need anything."

"Thanks, sweetie," Ben said. "Your mom laid out some of the bills for me, so I'll be going over this financial stuff."

"Better you than me," Bailey said, laughing.

"How do you get a horse at liberty to come to you in a pasture at a trot or a lope?" Bailey asked her mom. "I can get Nugget to come to me at a walk, but I don't know how to ask for the other gaits.

"It's not a simple answer," Annie responded. "Which as you already know is the case many times working with horses." Annie put a halter and lead rope on Raina.

"As you know, there are two main forces in working with horses: drive and draw," Annie explained.

"The first thing I would do is work on line asking my horse to back away from me and then come toward me," Annie said, as she demonstrated this with Raina. "Some folks call this exercise the 'boomerang' or 'yo-yo'. You face your horse and apply pressure with your core, raise your energy, then slightly wiggle the rope to create increased pressure to ask your horse to back up. You can also use your stick if necessary. The second she shifts her weight back, you release the pressure. You repeat this adding only enough pressure to be effective. The moment your horse does what you want, you release the pressure. You back her all the way to the end of the lead but leave some slack so she doesn't feel the weight of the rope causing her to come toward you yet. Wait for a bit and let her relax and soak. Then you lightly slide your hands toward yourself on the rope hand-over-hand, creating a slight pulling sensation to encourage the horse to come toward you again. When she comes in to you, you gently rub her."

"When this gets good online, you can go off line," said Annie, removing Raina's halter and lead.

"It's best to work on this in a smaller space," Annie continued, "like a round pen or paddock rather than a open pasture. In a small space you can always cross over and be faster than your horse if she tries to leave you. Your horse can leave you mentally, but can't really get too far away from you physically in a round pen."

Annie moved Raina's hind end over slightly by applying pressure. "Now that I have her head facing me, I back slightly to draw her to me at a walk," Annie said. "How do I get a horse to increase her speed?"

"By uping your phases or increasing the pressure," Bailey responded.

"Exactly, now if I increase the pressure by flicking the end of the rope toward Raina," Annie explained. "I am asking her to increase her speed. She may come toward me faster or she could turn and leave. She could also stop or continue coming at a walk. If she increases her speed, great, just remember to stop her with your energy about an arm's length from you. If she stops, repeat your request. She wasn't sure what to do. If she continues to come at a walk, up your energy and request. If she turns and leaves, you will need to cross over and get ahead of her to stop and turn her and get her with you again, or go back on line until she is less likely to leave you. It's best not to set a pattern with the horse that we don't want."

"That's a lot to remember, Mom," Bailey said. "I'm taking notes."

"As you can see, you have to constantly adjust to the situation as you go along," Annie added, "depending on what the horse does in response to your request. Remember, a horse only does what they think they are supposed to be doing. If things don't go as you thought they would, your horse probably didn't understand. Be clearer in your directions, and break it down into smaller pieces to make it easier for your horse."

"I can't believe how much I have to work on," Bailey commented, "as soon as my ankle heals."

"It helps when you can start reading the horse and know what she's thinking, by looking at the signs: ear position, where the horse is looking, soft eye or scared eye, head high or low, and tail position. When you are able to know the foot fall of the horse for each gait, then you have an idea which foot will move next. All of this put together gives you a great deal of insight into what the horse will do next.

"I'm not going to work further on this exercise with Raina," Annie said, "because we're not really ready for this yet. It's best to work in a progression of easy to difficult, and this exercise requires putting quite a few pieces together. I want to set her up for success, not failure. First I need to work more with her on each individual piece. The basics are: forward motion, direction, speed and moving each part of the horse."

"Will I ever be as good with horses as you, Mom?" Bailey asked.

"You are closer than you think, dear," Annie said. "You just have to keep working at it like you are now, and before you know it, you'll be there. Then you'll want to set new goals for yourself. Remember not to compare yourself to anyone else — try to be a little better each day than the day before."

"You make working with horses sound so easy," Bailey said. "Sometimes it feels easy, but a lot of times it feels really hard. I love it the most when I don't think about any of this, I'm just doing it. I'm in the middle of riding or working with Moses or Nugget on the ground, and I'm just with my horse. Everything flows and I feel wonderful!"

"That's the most important thing to remember — how you feel," Annie commented. "When you feel good, your horse does too!"

"Speaking of feeling good," Bailey said, "I should go check on Grandpa."

"Great idea," agreed Annie.

"Hi, Bailey," Ben said, as she walked into the room. "I'm really getting bored."

"Well, let's think about this," Bailey offered, "and see if we can come up with some ideas. I'm making lunch now."

"Sounds good," Ben said. "I'm hungry anyway."

"I'll help you to the kitchen," Bailey said.

"What about making some of your leather work, Grandpa?" Bailey asked. "Folks at church ask me and Mom if you have any bridles or breast collars for sale. They love your work."

"That would give me something to work on," Ben agreed. "It's no fun sitting around with nothing to do."

"Whatever you want to work on, Grandpa," Bailey said, "we'll help you get set-up to do. A couple weeks ago, you were talking about tying some new flies for fishing."

"I feel better already," Ben announced, a smile coming to his face. "Think, I'll start with some fly tying. When I feel good enough, I can even take the ATV to the stream and go fishing."

Annie and Ross came in for lunch and Ben told them about his plans.

"That's great, Dad," Annie said. "We'll help you set up everything. Also, Lucas just called me back. He's working over at the Goodwin's farm, but he gave me

Ethan McFadyen's name and number. Lucas said Ethan is honest and hard-working. He did haying for the Thomas family last year, but they don't need him this year. I called Ethan and he can start tomorrow."

"Let's give him a try," Ben said. "I trust Lucas's judgement."

"Ross, bring some hay samples in from the fields after lunch," Annie said, "that way Grandpa can look at them and tell us which fields to start on first."

"Okay, Mom," Ross said. "I'll do that right away."

"Charlie was going to come over tomorrow," Bailey said. "I'll call and ask her if she can come early and help."

"Good idea," said Annie, "we can use all the hands we can get."

"Mom, we're going to the potluck at church Sunday, right?" asked Bailey.

"Yes, I'm bringing a dish," replied Annie. "Although we may need to come back a little earlier than usual depending on where we are in the hay process."

"Okay, I invited Noah to come," Bailey said, piling tuna salad on her bread.

"Hey, wait a minute shrimp," Ross hollered, "save some for me!"

"Oops!" Bailey said surprised. "I got carried away. Take this Ross, I'll open another can and mix up some more."

"Thanks, Sis," Ross came back.

"I wish Dad was going to be home for the potluck," said Bailey.

"I wish he was too," Annie agreed, "but Sunday night will be here before you know it."

"How's the work coming, Ross?" Annie asked, while pouring herself a cup of coffee.

"The chores are going fine and fence repairs are done," Ross answered, "but I just can't get to working on that tree."

"Well don't worry about it," Annie suggested. "It's not going anywhere. You and your Dad will get it done after he gets home. We're doing very good on priorities and right now chores and haying are the priorities."

"Yes, ma'am," agreed Ross, and started laughing. "I guess I'm not the boss anymore!"

"Short reign of power, Ross," Bailey commented as they all laughed.

"Ethan will be here first thing in the morning," Annie said smiling. "The weather looks good for the next four days, so we can really make some progress!"

"Bring me those samples," Grandpa said, so I can tell which fields are ready to mow."

"I've got the plastic bags and permanent markers," said Ross, "so I can mark the field and section on each hay sample. I'll be back with them in a little while."

"Bailey and I will get your fly tying equipment," Annie said, "while Ross collects hay samples."

In the morning, as they were finishing breakfast, Bailey heard a truck pull in.

"It's probably Ethan," Annie said. Ross will you go out and let him know the plan? You and Ethan will do cutting while Charlie and I do chores. Ask if he wants coffee."

"Yeah, I'm grabbing coffee now," answered Ross.

"Charlie should be here soon," Bailey said. "I'll get some tea, that's what she likes. I'll be right out."

"We've got a full day ahead," said Annie, as she went out the door.

"Need anything, Grandpa?" Bailey hollered out the question.

"No, sweetie," Ben yelled back from the living room, "I'm good for now."

"Thanks for giving us a hand," Annie said to Charlie. "Don't your folks need you today?"

"They're going to start cutting hay tomorrow," Charlie replied, as they started mucking the stalls. "That's why they said yes to me coming."

"Tell your mom, thanks," Annie added.

"I sure will, Mrs. Mathews," Charlie smiled.

"Charlie, here's your tea," Bailey said. "I'll set it here."

"Thanks!" Charlie said. "I definitely need that!"

"I can run the hose out and fill stall buckets and the paddock troughs," Bailey offered.

"That will be a big help," Annie smiled.

"Ross and Ethan are mowing," Annie said to Charlie, "so, I can really use your help."

"Glad I can help, Mrs. Mathews," Charlie said.

They worked until breaking for lunch.

"Here are some more hay samples," Ross said, laying them on the table next to Ben.

"All of these are ready to mow," said Ben, checking them thoroughly.

"We'll be mowing all afternoon then," Ross said, "so we can take advantage of the good weather."

They munched on their sandwiches, drank loads of iced tea and talked at lunch. Charlie and Ethan were still talking as they headed back out to work.

The next two days were almost the same except Charlie was working at her family's farm. Ross and Ethan tedded hay, Annie and Bailey did chores and fixed meals. Ben checked the hay at every stage. It was hard work in the heat. Ross said, "Next winter, when it's 20 degrees and snowing, and I'm feeding hay to those fuzzy little faces, I'll remember just how hot it was the day we put up this hay." They ate, talked and laughed during meals, and fell exhausted into bed at night. Then got up early and started again the next day.

Chapter Nine

Sunday morning, Bailey and her mom left for church. Annie brought a tuna macaroni salad that she and Bailey made the night before. After the service, everyone went into the dining hall.

Bailey was sitting with Charlie when she saw Noah and his grandma walk in. They stood talking with Annie and Reverend Norris, then Noah looked around the room.

"I'm so glad you could come to the potluck," Bailey said smiling, as Noah walked up to where she was sitting with Charlie.

"I wouldn't have missed the chance to see you," he responded, smiling and looking into Bailey's eyes.

"Do you want to go riding together Tuesday in the afternoon?" Bailey asked, as she felt herself blushing. "My dad will be home late tonight and they will be baling hay tomorrow, so I think I can get away for the afternoon on Tuesday. I could meet you half-way."

"Sure, how's your ankle feeling?" Noah asked. "I see you're still using the crutches. Will you be able to ride?"

"It's feeling really good," she responded. "I'm still using the crutches just to give it extra time to heal. I don't think I really need them, and that's a couple more days away. I'll take it easy."

"My grandma told me about a shortcut from my place to Charlie's," Noah stated, "it's a lot quicker."

"I could meet you at Charlie's," Bailey offered, "it's not half-way."

"That sounds great," agreed Noah.

"I've been on that trail," Charlie said to Noah, "but I didn't know it went all the way to your house."

"Have some food," Bailey offered. "There's a lot to choose from, chili, casseroles, salad, sandwiches and desserts."

"How's your grandpa?" asked Noah.

"He's doing so much better," Bailey replied. "He's able to get around pretty well with the crutches on his own."

"That's great to hear," Noah said. "I'm going to see if Grandma wants anything," Noah said.

"He's so cute," Charlie said, squeezing Bailey's arm, after Noah had walked away.

"I know," Bailey agreed, grinning, "isn't he?"

"Noah really likes you," Charlie said to Bailey.

"Grandma's happy," Noah said to Bailey after coming back. "She already has a plate of food, and she's sitting with your mom."

"Eat," Bailey said, "then we'll introduce you to our friends. I think a local band is going to play some music. See, they're setting up over there."

"Cool, this is great!" Noah smiled, as he sat down with his plate of food.

"Who's playing?" Bailey asked Charlie.

"I think it's Todd and Allie's band," Charlie said. "There's Todd bringing in some of the equipment, now."

"Ross knows them better than I do," Bailey said. "He's heard them play many times."

"Noah this is my brother Zach and my sister Kerrie," Charlie said. "Guys, this is Noah Collins. Noah helped Bailey get help when her grandpa got hurt."

"Hey, let's go over and talk with Todd and Allie," Bailey suggested.

"What kind of music do they play?" asked Noah.

"They play Popular, Christian, Country and some original songs," replied Bailey, "a little bit of everything. I love their vocals."

"Come on, I'll introduce you," Kerrie said. "I know them from school."

"Todd and Allie, this is Noah Collins," Kerrie said. "He lives on the Wilburn side of the mountain.

This is Todd, Allie, Sam and Gabe. Their band is *River Lights*."

"Nice to meet you," Noah said, extending his hand to Todd. "I can't wait to hear you. I don't get to hear live bands very often. Do you play guitar?"

"Yes, Allie and I both play guitar, and sing," replied Todd. "Sam plays drums and Gabe's on bass. We all sing vocals. Do you play?"

"I play a little acoustic guitar," Noah replied, "but nothing like this, just for myself."

"Well, if you stick around," Todd offered, "toward the end we'll invite you to sit in. We have an extra guitar. I'll make sure it's tuned up."

"Oh, I don't think I could do it," remarked Noah, with a sigh. "I'd be too nervous."

"You'll be fine," Todd said. "That's the great thing about playing in a church – it's a very forgiving audience." Todd and Noah laughed, then they all laughed.

"You can do it," Bailey encouraged Noah. "Ross sits in with them on bass sometimes. He says it's fun!"

"Where is Ross?" Noah asked.

"He and Ethan are raking hay into windrows," Bailey replied. "They may start baling this afternoon. Mom hired Ethan to help out, with Grandpa and me out of commission and Dad away. We've been working really hard the last several days. Mom's been doing chores and I have been helping as much as I can with chores, preparing meals and being Grandpa's gofer."

"I'm sure it's been tough, but you make a good gofer," Noah said, smiling.

"I've been a perfect gofer on these crutches," Bailey laughed. "With Ethan helping and Dad coming home late tonight, we're making out okay!"

People had come around and cleared the tables. Now they were asking folks to get up and move some of the tables and chairs to make room to dance.

"It's too bad Grandpa couldn't come," Bailey interjected. "I'm sure he would love to see your grandma."

"Yes, they've got stories that go way back," Noah told Bailey.

"Grandpa said he would tell me some as soon as he's feeling better," Bailey said.

"Boy that road to get here is a long drive," Noah admitted, "Now I know why Gram, Gramp and Ben hadn't seen each other in years. It sure is a long way around."

"It's too bad the trail isn't a regular road or at least a wagon road," Bailey thought out loud. "It would be a lot easier traveling back and forth if it was in better shape."

"What a novel idea!" Noah said. "There's a project to work on."

"I was only thinking out loud," Bailey laughed. "It

sounds like an awful lot of work to me!"

"Maybe, maybe not," Noah added. "Let's check out the trail between my house and Charlie's and see what that's like."

"That sounds like a plan," Bailey smiled. Noah smiled back. Bailey suddenly realized that she liked Noah very much.

At that moment, Todd's voice came over the microphone saying, "Hi, my name is Todd and we're *River Lights*." He introduced the band members and added, "Please feel free to sing along or get up and dance."

"Bailey, it's time to go," Annie said walking over to where she was sitting. "We really need to get back to help with afternoon chores. The boys and your grandpa will be getting hungry and your Dad will be arriving home later."

"The band's about to start," Bailey said, "and I'd really like to stay awhile."

"We can bring her home," Charlie offered.

"Okay, as long as your mom doesn't mind," Annie responded.

"She won't mind," Charlie stated.

"I've really enjoyed seeing you after so many years," Sarah said to Annie.

"Me too, Sarah," Annie replied. "Let's get together again soon."

"Give my best to Ben," Sarah said.

"I will," answered Annie, giving her a hug.

"Grandma, would you like to dance?" Noah asked Sarah. The band began playing a beautiful slow song and people were getting up to dance.

"I'd love to dear," Sarah answered. "It's been years since I've danced."

Noah got up, took his grandma's hand and led her to the dance floor. Sarah had a smile on her face, as she danced with her grandson. Bailey noticed how much Noah cared for her.

"I cleared it with Beth," Annie said. "See you at the house later. Have fun!"

"Thanks, Mom," Bailey called after her.

"Finally, I can talk to you alone," Charlie said to Bailey. "Do you know if Ethan has a girlfriend?"

"I don't have a clue," Bailey answered.

"I didn't get to spend much time with him the other day," Charlie said, "but he seemed so nice. I think he's super hot."

"Ooh, Charlie has a crush," Bailey teased.

"Well, maybe a little," Charlie laughed.

"Come over tomorrow," Bailey suggested. "Eventhough my Dad's coming home tonight, I think Mom asked Ethan to work a few more days to help us catch up with all the work."

"That would be great!" Charlie agreed, as they both giggled. "We will be haying too, but I'll think of some reason to get away for awhile."

"Can I use your phone?" Bailey asked. "I forgot to

ask my mom what time Dad's getting home. I want to be there. I *so* wish I had my own phone."

"Sure," Charlie answered, handing Bailey her phone. "That's it! Don't give it back to me," Charlie said.

"What?" Bailey asked, as she called. "Mom, what time is Dad getting home?" "Okay, I'll be there. See you later."

"I'll have to ride over tomorrow to get my phone!" answered Charlie.

"Oh, right!" Bailey laughed. "You mad sorcerer! That'll work!"

"What are you two laughing about?" Noah asked.

"Oh, just family stuff," Charlie claimed, still chuckling.

"Where's your grandma?" asked Bailey.

"She's catching up with some old friends, Tom and Joan Weaver, who used to live in Wilburn," Noah replied. "She hasn't seen them in years."

"Is she having a good time?" Bailey asked.

"Yes, she's so glad we came," Noah answered. "Grandma taught me how to dance," he said, with a smile. "I think she was checking me out to see how much I remembered."

"Oh, I saw her face," Bailey commented. "Your grandma was so pleased and totally enjoyed the dance."

"Do you think you can manage a dance?" Noah

asked. "I don't want you to risk reinjuring your ankle though."

"Not this dance," Bailey said, "it's too fast. Can we wait for a slow one?"

"Definitely," Noah replied.

"I love to dance to anything, fast or slow," Bailey added. "I just don't want to chance it. The band definitely has it together, don't you think?" Bailey asked.

"Yeah, Todd plays some wicked leads," Noah replied, "and their harmonies are fantastic."

"Here's a slow one," Noah said, raising his eyebrows. "What do you think?"

"Let's try it," Bailey responded, smiling.

Noah stood and took Bailey by the hand and they walked to the dance floor. He held her softly as they swayed to the music. Bailey could feel his breath on her right ear. She felt like her heart would fly right out of her chest, but at the same time she felt calm, safe and happy. She had never felt like this in her whole life. Then she remembered riding Nugget and loping through the pasture — two heartbeats and four feet flying together. She thought to herself, "It does feel kind of similar." She didn't want the moment to end.

Bailey felt Noah gently guiding her. "Dancing is very similar to riding and working with horses," she said, sounding almost surprised. She didn't realize she was talking out loud.

"What do you mean?" Noah asked.

"You're trying to tell me how you want me to move using body language, energy and feel," Bailey replied. "You're communicating to me; direction with your core and eyes; speed with your energy; and refining it all with the pressure of your hands on my hand and waist."

"That's so interesting!" Noah exclaimed, "I never thought about dancing that way!"

"It's easy to follow you," Bailey said, "because you're very clear and gentle with your cues."

"Thank you," Noah said. "I didn't even realize how I was doing this."

"I hadn't thought about dancing in this way either," Bailey commented, "until now."

"They're starting to play a fast song," Noah said.

"Can we sit this one out?" Bailey asked.

"Sure," Noah replied.

"Some of our friends are sitting with Charlie," Bailey said. "I'll introduce you. Hey everyone, this is Noah Collins."

"Hi, Noah," the group said.

"Noah, this is Robbie, Shana, Lily, Josh and Corey." Bailey said.

"Hey," Noah said, "nice to meet you."

The group sat talking, getting to know each other better and listening to the music, for quite a while. Todd announced over the microphone, "Let's get

Noah up here to sit in on guitar."

"Go ahead, Noah," Bailey said, reassuringly, "you'll do fine."

Noah stood up and walked toward the band.

Todd handed a guitar to Noah. "We'll start with something easy," he said. "How about *Be Thou My Vision* in the key of C?"

Noah nodded, "Okay."

"*Be Thou My Vision,*" Todd announced into the mike. "Everyone please sing along, the words are up on the screen behind me."

Allie led the singing and almost everyone joined in. Bailey saw Noah starting to relax. She thought the fact that the audience was singing took a lot of pressure off him. She noticed Todd saying something to Noah on the side.

"Are you ready to try a lead for one verse?" Todd asked Noah.

"Sure," Noah nodded.

"Noah on lead," Todd said, through the mike. The screen turned off, so the singing stopped.

Bailey listened as Noah played a beautiful lilting lead that had a lot of feeling in it, while the rest of the band backed him up. "Oooh, that was nice!" she whispered to Charlie.

"That boy has skills!" Charlie whispered, smiling.

"He sure does!" Bailey agreed, smiling back.

The verse was finished, the screen came back on

and everyone started singing again.

After the song ended, Todd spoke into the mike, "We're going to pick it up with a fast dance song. Come on now, everyone back on the dance floor."

"Want to keep playing?" Todd asked aside to Noah.

"Sure," Noah nodded.

Robbie and Shana got up and danced. Bailey, Charlie and their friends talked, laughed and enjoyed the music. Bailey could see Noah smiling as he played. A few songs later Lily and Josh got up and danced.

Bailey noticed the time. "Can we leave for home soon?" Bailey said to Charlie. "I want to get home before my dad arrives."

"I'll go talk to my mom," Charlie answered.

The song *River Lights* was playing finished. Bailey approached Noah, "We're going to be leaving soon."

"Okay," Noah said to Bailey. "I'm going to take a break," he said to Todd, as he stood up and propped the guitar against the chair.

"Let's have a round of applause for Noah," Todd said into the mike, "thanks for joining us."

"I was having so much fun," Noah said. "I didn't realize how long I'd been playing."

"I'm glad you played," Bailey responded. "You're so talented, I love your leads."

"I wanted to spend time with you," Noah said.

"It's okay," Bailey smiled, "we'll see each other Tuesday, when we go riding."

"Noah, you played beautifully," Sarah said, as she walked up to them. "I hate to cut this short, but we have a long drive ahead."

"I guess we're all getting ready to leave," Noah said to Bailey.

"I didn't even get a chance to talk with you Mrs. Collins," said Bailey.

"That's all right, dear," Sarah said. "I wanted Noah to spend time with you young folks. We'll get a chance to talk another time." Sarah hugged Bailey, "I'm so glad we came. Please tell your grandpa hello for me, and tell him I hope he heals quickly."

"I will," Bailey said.

"Thanks for inviting me," Noah said to Bailey. "I'll see you Tuesday." Noah turned and said to his new friends, "hope to see you all again soon."

On their way out, Bailey could see Noah talking to Todd and Allie. The band had taken a break, so they were relaxing for a few minutes.

After Noah and Sarah left, Bailey also noticed how the room felt different. She was already looking forward to Tuesday.

"Come on, let's hit the road," Charlie said, taking Bailey by the arm. "You can tell me all about him on the ride home."

Chapter Ten

"Mom, I'm home!" Bailey called, bursting through the kitchen door.

"She's out in the barn," Ben called from the family room.

"Oh, hi, Grandpa, how are you feeling?" Bailey asked, as she went into the room. "Do you need anything?"

"No thanks, I just managed to get myself some coffee and a piece of pie," Ben said. "How was the potluck?"

"I had a really great time!" Bailey answered. "All my friends were there, Noah plays guitar and was asked to sit in with the band!" she said, practically bubbling over. "It was so much fun! Oh, Mrs. Collins came with Noah," Bailey added. "She said to say hi, and she hopes you get better real soon."

"Too bad about this broken leg," Ben said, "I

would have gone to the potluck. It would be so nice to see her."

"I'm sure we'll see her again soon," Bailey said. "I'm going out to see if Mom needs any help before Dad gets home."

"I expect he'll be here any time now," Ben said.

"Mom, I'm here," Bailey shouted entering the barn. "Do you need any help?"

"Actually, Ross and I are just finishing up," Annie answered. "Sit down on that bale and tell me all that happened after I left."

"Oh Mom, I had such a great time!" Bailey said, grinning again. "Noah and I danced just one slow dance. Don't worry, I took it extremely easy on my ankle. Noah's a good dancer...and guess what?

"What, honey?" Annie asked.

"Noah plays guitar. The band asked him to sit in and he played really good. Charlie and I hung out with our friends while he played, and Mrs. Collins visited with some old friends she knew from Wilburn. It was so much *fun*!...and now *Dad* will be home!"

"Isn't it wonderful?" Annie asked.

"Yes, it is," Bailey agreed. "A few days ago, time seemed to be dragging and now time is *flying*!"

They talked and laughed while Annie finished the chores. Ross finished up the outside chores, then they all went to the house.

"I'm getting everything lined up for dinner," Annie said. "We'll eat when your dad arrives."

"We'll wash up and set the table," Bailey said to Ross.

"I hear a car pulling in," Ross called out. "Dad's home!"

"Perfect timing." Annie smiled.

Ross was the first one out the door. "Dad, Dad," he called, "you're here!" They hugged and slapped each other on the back.

"Dad, I missed you so much!" Bailey called, following on the crutches.

"I've been hearing amazing things about you young lady," Will said, as he put his arms around Bailey.

"Oh, Dad," Bailey sighed, "It's been so hard, and so many things have happened. I don't know where to start." Bailey loved getting hugged by her dad, "It seems like you've been gone forever!

"We'll talk more at dinner, sweetie," Will said. "First, I have something special for you." He reached into a bag and pulled out something and handed it to Bailey.

"A phone, *my own phone*!" Bailey exclaimed, as she dropped one crutch and practically danced around.

"Well, you took on a great deal of responsibility," Will said, congratulating her. "It sounds like things would have been a lot easier for you and Grandpa if you had had your own phone. Your mom and I both realize now how important it is that you have one."

"Thanks, Dad," Bailey said hugging her dad again, almost in tears. "This means *so much* to me. I can't even begin to say how much. She said, now smiling, "I can't believe it, *yay!*"

"You deserve it, Sis," Ross said, smiling.

They went into the house where Annie and Ben were waiting. "Will, you're finally here," Annie said as they hugged and kissed, "thank God. I've missed you, we've all missed you."

"I know, honey," Will said, "I can take over some of the burden and work now."

"Ben how are you feeling?" Will asked.

"A little better every day," Ben answered.

They ate, talked, laughed and shared the stories of the past weeks, till fairly late. They enjoyed the evening together until they remembered that they were baling hay in the morning, and then quickly went to bed.

In the morning, the breakfast table was a beehive of talk and activity. Annie and Will fixed breakfast for everyone. Ross and Bailey set the table and poured juice and coffee.

"Ooooh, buckwheat banana pancakes," Bailey smiled, "you made my favorite, thanks Dad."

"Ross, Ethan and I will do the haying," Will said, after they were all seated. "Annie, with Bailey's help, will do the chores. Annie, time permitting, will work horses. Bailey will fix lunch for everyone.

"I guess I'm not 'Ross the Boss' anymore," interjected Ross, laughing.

"What?" Will asked.

"While you were away, we took turns doing the schedule in the morning," Ross answered.

"That sounds like fun," Will said, "we'll have to make that part of our routine."

"I'll help Bailey fix lunch," Ben said. "I'm sick of sitting around and not doing my share."

"Dad, your leg is broken," Annie said, "you need to keep your weight off it so your leg will heal properly."

"I know. I'm getting pretty good at using these crutches though," Ben said. "I won't put any weight on my leg."

"Dad, I wish you would take it easy" Annie said, "please be careful."

"I will dear," Ben said.

"Hi folks," Ethan said, as he came through the door.

"Have some breakfast, Ethan," Annie offered, handing him a plate.

"Thanks, Mrs. Mathews," Ethan said, as he grabbed the plate and pulled up a chair. "I didn't eat breakfast yet."

"Is it okay if I meet Noah at Charlie's tomorrow afternoon?" Bailey asked. "His grandma told him about a shorter trail from his place to Charlie's and he wants to check it out."

"I don't think you should ride with that ankle yet." Annie said.

"It's just about all better," Bailey exclaimed. "I won't put any weight on it, promise...and I'll take it really easy."

"Okay, but no posting," Annie said very firmly. "I don't want you reinjuring your ankle."

"Thanks, Mom," Bailey smiled, "I'll be very careful."

"We want you healthy," Will added. "It's important with injuries to go back to activities gradually. Ben it's going to take your leg much longer to heal. We all have to take care of ourselves and each other."

"All right," Ben said, "I'll give it more time. I'm just used to being more active."

"We need your help in many ways, Ben," Will said. "Annie told me you've been paying the bills, ordering supplies and helping with the planning. Of course, your farming knowledge is invaluable. We need you checking the readiness of the hay at every step. We couldn't run this place without you."

"Thanks, Will, I guess I needed to hear that," Ben said.

"We want to hear your ideas and when you're bored," Will added, "so we can help you get through this healing process as fast as possible."

"That sounds good to me," Ben added, laughing, "although if you ask me, it couldn't be fast enough." They all laughed.

"Let's get to work everyone," Will announced.

They all went out except Bailey, who stayed behind to clean up the kitchen and get Grandpa some coffee. Bailey wondered what time Charlie would come to pick up her phone. When she finished, Bailey went to the barn to help her mom with the chores.

"Well, that just about does it for the morning chores," Annie said, later on.

"I'll go in," Bailey said, "and get lunch ready."

"Thanks," Annie said, "I'll be along in a few minutes."

"We're starved." Will exclaimed, as he and the boys filed in for lunch. "Nothing gets your appetite going like baling hay. We'll wash up first."

"There's potato salad and all the fixings for sandwiches," Bailey said. "Help yourselves and make your own plate. Everything's on the counter. I already poured ice tea for everyone."

As they were sitting down, Charlie came in. "Hey

Bailey," Charlie said, "I forgot to get my phone back from you yesterday."

"It's in the other room," Bailey said. "I'll get it."

"Charlie, have you had lunch yet?" Annie asked. "Grab a plate and join us."

"Thanks, Mrs. Mathews, no, I haven't," Charlie replied, while getting a plate.

"How's it going?" Ben asked Will.

"We've got a pretty good system going," Will answered. "We already put up about 200 bales."

Ross and Ethan were laughing about their bale stacking contest. They each said they won.

"Do you attend public school?" Charlie asked Ethan.

"I'm home schooled, answered Ethan. "I've been haying different farms about four seasons now, saving up money for college."

"What are you planning to study?" asked Charlie.

"Sustainable ranching and ranch management," Ethan replied.

"My brother Zach wants to study ranch management too," Charlie commented.

"Do you ever go to the potluck gatherings at the church?" Ethan asked.

"Noah, Bailey and I, and other friends, were there yesterday!" Charlie exclaimed, smiling. We had a super time, there was a band too. You should go sometime."

"I wanted to go," Ethan explained, "but I won't be

able to until haying is done for the season."

"We had so much fun," Bailey interjected. "Ross couldn't go either because of haying."

"Speaking of haying," Will said, "we should get back to work."

"I've got to get back to help with our haying too," Charlie said. "Thanks for lunch. See you soon, Bailey."

The day's work went smoothly and over 400 bales of hay were put in the barn. That evening around the dinner table they laughed and talked about all they had accomplished.

There was breakfast the next morning, and then chores. All morning, Bailey was thinking about meeting Noah at Charlie's house for a ride.

"Ross will you saddle Nugget for me after lunch?" Bailey asked, while they were eating. "I still shouldn't be lifting heavy things. I already groomed him."

"Sure, kid," Ross answered. "That's right, you're riding to Charlie's."

"I might be gone most of the afternoon," Bailey said.

"Go, have fun," Annie said, "Just take care of that ankle, and be sure to take your phone."

"No worries, Mom," Bailey said, "that phone's not

leaving my side."

Everyone laughed.

Bailey bridled Nugget and asked him to move in every way, hind end, shoulders, forward, backward, left, right and sideways, to make sure he was listening to her. She mounted up and they stood for a few moments, while she rubbed him all over.

"It feels good to be with you again," she said to Nugget, "and riding again." Bailey leaned forward, hugging him and breathing in his scent. Horses always smelled like hay and sunshine to her. She sat back in the saddle and relaxed into the feel. This was one of the places she loved to be the most. She gently asked Nugget to walk and suddenly realized how free she felt. The sun sparkled as it glinted off the sand and bits of quartz in the road. The trees and grass, everything around her seemed bright and new. She loved living on the mountain. Bailey breathed in the clean mountain air and thought, "There's no better place on the face of the earth."

Nugget easily maintained an even walk, he was alert and paying attention, but relaxed. When she reached the place where the rock slide had happened, she stopped and took a close look at where the road crew had worked. There were mounds of rock and debris piled up on the side and they had positioned some boulders to help hold it in place.

In no time, they reached Charlie's house. Bailey

dismounted, removed Nugget's bridle, hung it over the saddle horn and allowed him to munch grass.

"Hello, Charlie," Bailey called out, as she knocked on the door.

"Hey," Charlie answered, opening the door.

"Look, my new phone!" Bailey said excitedly, holding it out for Charlie to see.

"Congrats!" Charlie exclaimed, "nice!"

The two sat talking for a few minutes. "Here's Noah now," Bailey said looking up.

"I can't ride with you two," Charlie said. "I've got to help bale and stack this afternoon. In fact, I've got to get back out there now. See you later!"

"Hey," Noah called to Bailey. Then he told Gus, "Whoa," riding up close to where Bailey was sitting.

"I'm ready to go," Bailey said, putting Nugget's bridle back on.

"How is your grandpa?" Noah asked. "I see you rode Nugget again today. How is Moses?"

"Grandpa's feeling a lot better, thanks," answered Bailey. "The swelling has gone down in Moses' leg, but I wanted to give him more time to heal."

"That's good news!" Noah said. "The trail over was shorter and more even. It was clear, no trees down and I could trot a good part of the way and even lope a bit."

"That's good news, too!" Bailey said, as she swung up into the saddle, from the off side. "It's great having my dad home. Look, he got me a phone," she said, holding it up.

"More good news!" Noah smiled.

"Now we can keep in touch," they both said at the same time, smiling and laughing.

They turned and walked off down the dirt road that ran along the edge of one of the Anderson's pastures. The road was nice and even.

"Want to lope?" Bailey asked.

"Are you okay to lope?" Noah asked. "I noticed you mounted on the off side."

"Yes," Bailey nodded. "I'll slow down if I need to. I guess mounting on the off side is just getting to be a habit."

They both picked up a nice slow lope, and looked at each other and smiled. Bailey's heart was soaring and she thought, "four hearts beating and eight legs flying."

Made in the USA
Lexington, KY
02 September 2018